The story of an innocent man caught in a deadly conspiracy has been told before, but Lee Goldberg takes it a step further in this rollicking, sometimes humorous, always deadly *True Fiction*. Highly recommended."
—Brendan DuBois, author of *Storm Cell*

PRAISE FOR *TRUE FICTI*

"Thriller fiction at its absolute finest—and it could ha
But not to me, I hope."
—Lee Child, #1 *New York Times* bestselling autho
Jack Reacher series

"This may be the most fun you'll ever have reading a tl
breathtaking rush of suspense, intrigue, and laughter th
Goldberg could pull off. I loved it."
—Janet Evanovich, #1 *New York Times* bestselling ;

"This is my life . . . in a thriller! *True Fiction* is grea
—Brad Meltzer, #1 *New York Times* bestselling autl
House of Secrets

"A conspiracy thriller of the first order, a magical blen
and it-could-happen scary fiction. Nail-biting, page-tur
laced with Goldberg's wry humor, *True Fiction* is a true
reminiscent of *Three Days of the Condor* and the best of H
innocent man-in-peril films."
—Paul Levine, bestselling author of *Bum Rap*

"Great fun that moves as fast as a jet. Goldberg walks a ti
between suspense and humor and never slips."
—Linwood Barclay, *New York Times* bestselling autho
The Twenty-Three

"I haven't read anything this much fun since Donald E. We
comic-caper novels. Immensely entertaining, clever, and ti
—David Morrell, *New York Times* bestselling author of *Mur*
Fine Art and *First Blood*

TRUE
FICTION

OTHER TITLES BY LEE GOLDBERG

Fire & Ice (with Jude Hardin)
Carnival of Death (with Bill Crider)
Freaks Must Die (with Joel Goldman)
Slaves to Evil (with Lisa Klink)
The Midnight Special (with Phoef Sutton)
The Death Match (with Christa Faust)
The Black Death (with Aric Davis)
The Killing Floor (with David Tully)
Colder Than Hell (with Anthony Neil Smith)
Evil to Burn (with Lisa Klink)
Streets of Blood (with Barry Napier)
Crucible of Fire (with Mel Odom)
The Dark Need (with Stant Litore)
The Rising Dead (with Stella Greene)
Reborn (with Kate Danley, Phoef Sutton, and Lisa Klink)

The Jury Series

Judgment
Adjourned
Payback
Guilty

Nonfiction

The Best TV Shows You Never Saw
Unsold Television Pilots 1955–1989
Television Fast Forward
Science Fiction Filmmaking in the 1980s
(cowritten with William Rabkin, Randy Lofficier, and Jean-Marc Lofficier)
The Dreamweavers: Interviews with Fantasy Filmmakers of the 1980s
(cowritten with William Rabkin, Randy Lofficier, and Jean-Marc Lofficier)
Successful Television Writing (cowritten with William Rabkin)

TRUE FICTION

AN IAN LUDLOW THRILLER

LEE GOLDBERG

THOMAS & MERCER

Text copyright © 2018 by Adventures in Television, Inc.
All rights reserved.

Published by Thomas & Mercer, Seattle

www.apub.com

Amazon, the Amazon logo, and Thomas & Mercer are trademarks of Amazon.com, Inc., or its affiliates.

ISBN-13: 9781503949188 (hardcover)
ISBN-10: 1503949184 (hardcover)
ISBN-13: 9781503954076 (paperback)
ISBN-10: 1503954072 (paperback)

Cover design by Damon Freeman

Printed in the United States of America

First edition

For Valerie & Maddie, as always.

CHAPTER ONE

Honolulu. July 17. Noon. Hawaii-Aleutian Standard Time.

The assassin wore only a Speedo and his lean body was slathered with sunscreen that made him smell like a baked coconut. His name was Doric Thane and he sat on a poolside chaise lounge that faced Waikiki. To his right, and in the distance, was Honolulu International Airport. Behind him, the hotel tower stood against the backdrop of Diamond Head volcano and pale kids with floaties around their chubby arms frolicked loudly in the overchlorinated pool. There was a closed MacBook on his lap and a cold lava flow cocktail on the table beside him. He scratched absently at the puckered gunshot scar on his stomach and sighed with contentment.

Thane opened his MacBook and a detailed simulation of an airplane cockpit control panel filled his screen. The photo-realistic animated graphic looked identical to the actual control panel in the cockpit of TransAmerican Flight 976, which at that very moment was preparing to depart from Honolulu filled with sunburned tourists in loud aloha shirts and board shorts heading back to Cleveland.

Captain Avery Jenkins went through his preflight checklist. He had a touch of gray at his temples that conveyed stability, experience, and wisdom. Those were qualities that every passenger wanted to see in a pilot and for some stupid reason, the patches of gray bestowed it all upon him. So he'd begun coloring his hair years before the gray came naturally. Jenkins had a new first officer on this flight, Billy Shoop, who was busy plugging coordinates into the flight management system. Shoop was youthful enough to regularly get carded at bars and looked like he had second-degree burns on his face. The captain saw traces of his younger self in Shoop and it made him a bit wistful.

"First layover in Hawaii?" Jenkins asked.

Shoop nodded. "How did you know?"

"Lucky guess. Let me share a little captainly advice. Next time you're here, don't fall asleep on the beach."

"I didn't. I'm very fair skinned. I get burned if someone aims a flashlight at me."

"Then we'd better get you back to Ohio before you burst into flames," Jenkins said. "You're taking us up. Let's get push clearance."

"Yes, sir." Shoop radioed the tower. "Honolulu Ground, TransAmerican 976 requests push clearance off Gate 4."

The air traffic controller responded right away, his voice as flat and emotionless as an automated recording. "TransAmerican 976, you're cleared to push. Advise when ready to taxi."

⊕

Five miles due south, from a chaise lounge at the Diamond Head Tradewinds Resort, the assassin studied the live readings on the airplane control console on his MacBook screen. TransAmerican Flight 976 was leaving the gate.

Doric Thane smiled. The fun was about to begin.

TransAmerican Flight 976 taxied to the runway and First Officer Shoop dutifully waited for the go-ahead from the tower.

"You are cleared for immediate liftoff on Runway 8R," the controller said by rote. "On departure, fly heading 140."

The runway was on a reef that pointed at the resorts along Waikiki, so the controllers always ordered departing planes, no matter where they were bound, to immediately head south to avoid buzzing the beach and destroying the tropical tranquility for the tourists.

"Roger. TransAmerican 976 cleared for takeoff on Runway 8R, heading 140," Shoop confirmed, then looked to the captain for the official confirmation.

"You have the aircraft," Jenkins said.

"I have the aircraft." Shoop sat up straight in his seat, confident and eager, and pushed the thrust levers forward and activated the auto-throttle.

The plane raced down the runway, picking up speed. Shoop pulled back the sidestick and the plane began climbing into the sky at two thousand feet per minute toward Diamond Head in the distance, where Doric Thane sat on his chaise lounge, his fingers poised over the keyboard of the MacBook on his lap.

The assassin tapped a few keys, initiating the autopilot on his cockpit console, stopping the climb and changing the flight's heading to 090. He was in control of the flight. The cockpit crew was as powerless as the passengers now. They might as well order a drink, eat some peanuts, and enjoy the ride.

Captain Jenkins instantly noticed that the plane was flying parallel to Honolulu on their left rather than veering to their right toward the open sea. But that wasn't all that was wrong. The altimeter showed them leveling off at twelve hundred feet when they should have been climbing.

"What are you doing?" Jenkins asked Shoop. "The heading is 140."

"I know that," Shoop said, struggling with his sidestick. "But the stick isn't responding."

The reason why was obvious. The captain saw that the green autopilot light was lit up on the instrument panel, indicating that the system had been activated. He sighed with irritation at the kid's carelessness. "That's because you accidentally engaged the autopilot."

Chagrined, Shoop pressed the autopilot button on his sidestick to disengage the system. But the light stayed on.

He shot the captain a frightened look. "It won't turn off."

"TransAmerican 976, turn immediately to 140," the controller yelled into his ear, some life in his voice now. "You have leveled off. I repeat, turn to 140."

Jenkins grasped his sidestick and hit the disconnect button, too. But the autopilot didn't disengage and his sidestick wouldn't respond, either. It didn't make any sense. He felt his heart drop into his stomach like a sandbag.

Thane saw the plane in the distance, heading his way like an obedient dog returning to its master. He typed in a new heading: 010 degrees.

The captain and the first officer were both pulling hard on their sidesticks, desperate to get a response, when the aircraft inexplicably turned east toward the high-rise hotels of Waikiki and began a fast, steady descent. The action meant more to Jenkins than an unexpected and terrifying navigational change. It was the cold touch of an unseen hand.

"Tell the tower we have an emergency," Jenkins ordered Shoop and continued to hit the autopilot button while he wrestled with the sidestick. "I have the aircraft."

The captain wasn't saying he had regained control. He was stating that he was now the only one attempting to fly the plane. This acknowledgment prevented two people from trying to fly the plane at the same time.

But that was exactly what was happening.

"Mayday, Mayday. TransAmerican 976 is declaring an emergency," Shoop said, his voice cracking. "We are not in control of the aircraft."

"But someone is," Jenkins said.

Shoop looked at him, baffled. "What do you mean?"

"We leveled off before the turn. That's a decision, not a computer glitch."

The captain was right about that.

⌖

The plane was heading straight for Waikiki. Thane could see it from where he was sitting. So could the tourists on chaise lounges around him. The tourists were getting to their feet, staring at the sky. Even the kids in the pools were beginning to realize something was very wrong. All eyes were fixed on the plane. Nobody noticed what was on the assassin's MacBook screen. He tapped the up arrow on his keyboard, increasing the plane's airspeed to 350 knots.

Now the people on Waikiki Beach could see and hear the plane coming in fast and low, only a hundred feet off the ground. Thousands of people on the sand scrambled in sheer terror, with no idea where to go. Thane saw the mass panic from afar. It reminded him of when he was a kid and liked to drop lit matches into anthills.

In the airplane's cockpit, Shoop was frozen by the sight of the rapidly approaching Honolulu skyline in front of him. But for Captain Jenkins, time slowed down and his mind cleared, even as the frantic air traffic controller was screaming "Pull up! Pull up!" in his ear and the altitude alarm wailed. He was focused on the problem. The autopilot had control of the plane. Someone had control of the autopilot. How could he stop it? The answer was so simple.

Kill the technology.

Jenkins hit a slew of buttons, shutting down all of the plane's computer systems. The system reverted to manual control and then he was flying an old-fashioned stick-and-rudder airplane. He felt the sidestick come alive in his hand like a startled, pissed-off animal.

"I have the plane!" he yelled.

Jenkins pulled back the stick, lifting the plane into a steep climb. But he didn't see any blue sky in front him. All he saw was the twentieth floor of the Hyatt Regency. It was too late.

The fuselage plowed right through the center of the hotel in an enormous fireball and the aircraft's wings were sheared off by the adjoining buildings. A chain reaction of explosions erupted as the flaming wreckage and toppled buildings spread the destruction inland. A massive, roiling cloud of fire, glass, and rubble sprawled out in all directions, covering the beach and sending people rushing into the water in a futile effort to escape the devastation.

The ground beneath Doric Thane shook as if the long-dead Diamond Head volcano were about to blow. Panic broke out among the people around him, which he thought was stupid, since they were obviously a safe distance from the crash and the death cloud. Instead, they should have been celebrating their good luck.

The assassin closed his MacBook, tucked it under one arm, and got to his feet, observed by no one amid all the senseless screaming and crying. He picked up his cocktail and was pleased to discover that it hadn't lost its chill. He walked casually away, his back to the terrified tourists and the carnage, and sipped his lava flow. It was cold and sweet.

This was how to kill people.

CHAPTER TWO

Seattle, Washington. July 17. 3:00 p.m. Pacific Standard Time.

The impeccably tailored Tom Ford tuxedo fit Clint Straker's muscular, six-foot frame like a second skin and showed no sign of the two knives and the garrote sewn into the lining. He was one of the two hundred guests at a garden party on the back lawn of international shipping magnate Martin Hung's massive lakefront estate. They were all there to honor Hung on his fifty-fifth birthday. Straker was there to make sure Hung didn't celebrate his fifty-sixth.

"Hung may be the leader of the world's largest sex slavery ring but you have to admire his beautiful home and its feng shui," said Kenny Wu, Straker's local contact and the man who'd secured him an invitation to the party. Wu's tuxedo was one size too big for his bony body and made him look like a ridiculously overdressed scarecrow. "See how the house is tucked into the hillside and faces the water? That creates an unobstructed path for the chi."

Straker's gaze was on a beautiful Asian woman in a white dress so sheer that she might as well have been wearing nothing at all. "Chi?"

"The positive life force."

"Good to know," Straker said and picked up two full champagne glasses from a passing waiter. "Be seeing you, Wu."

"Where are you going?"

Straker tipped his head toward the woman. "To create an unobstructed path for my chi."

Ian Ludlow finished reading aloud from his book and smiled, pleased with the last line and with himself for being clever enough to write it. He stood at a wobbly lectern beside a table covered with hardcover copies of his latest Clint Straker thriller, *The Dead Never Forget*, and paperback copies of the previous six titles in his *New York Times* bestselling series. His book covers all featured the silhouette of his gun-toting action hero set against a backdrop of explosions, international landmarks, sports cars, and beautiful women with enormous boobs.

He was in Seattle, the first stop in a six-city, ten-day publicity tour for his new book. Today he was speaking at a boho-chic bookstore where everybody reeked of weed and only eight people showed up for his signing. Ian didn't care about the low turnout. He was on a paid vacation.

"I think that excerpt sums up the essence of Clint Straker and what makes him so attractive to men and women alike," Ian told his audience, who sat scattered among the four rows of chairs in front of him. "Any questions?"

A young guy in a faded University of Washington sweatshirt spoke up. "How much do you share in common with Clint Straker?"

"Isn't it obvious?" Ian asked the audience. "Look at me."

They did. What they saw was a guy on the dark side of thirty with the soft body of someone whose idea of exercise was walking into McDonald's rather than using the drive-through. His right arm was in a blue cast and locked at a ninety-degree angle but he wasn't wearing a sling. Instead, he just hooked his right thumb in the gap above one of the closed buttons of his untucked dress shirt to support the weight of his broken arm. He wore fashionably faded jeans and white Nikes. By contrast, Clint Straker was physically perfect, a six-foot-tall Special Forces vet who looked great wearing anything and could be mistaken for the model for Michelangelo's *David* when he wore nothing at all. He was a spy for hire, a deductive genius and an unstoppable killing machine who didn't salute any flag or fight for any political or religious ideology except his own personal moral code.

"Clint Straker can beat up three ninjas using only a napkin as a weapon," Ian said. "But I've never hit anybody in my life and I'm a complete klutz. A few weeks ago, I accidentally blew up my house."

Which was a big reason why he was glad to be on a book tour. He was going to be living out of a suitcase for a while and he much preferred to do it at his publisher's expense rather than his own. While he was on tour, they paid for his accommodations and his meals, too. It was a sweet deal and the timing was perfect. He wondered if there was a way to extend the tour another week or two.

"So where did Clint come from?" the young man asked.

"Out of misery and desperation. I was in my third year as a writer on the TV series *Hollywood & the Vine*—"

The words were barely out of his mouth when someone interrupted and intoned, in a deep announcer's voice: "Half man, half plant, all cop."

Some people laughed and then it seemed like everybody in the store started singing the show's theme song, which was basically the chorus of Marvin Gaye's "I Heard It Through the Grapevine" with very different lyrics.

Ooooh you heard about that cop Vine
A plant who can't stand crime
You get caught, you're gonna do time . . .
Honey, honey yeah . . .

Ian smiled good-naturedly and looked at the back of the room to see how this newfound attention was playing with Vince, the scraggly-bearded store manager, and Margo, the twentysomething "author escort" with short-cropped deep-black hair who'd been hired by his publisher to drive him around Seattle. Vince looked as if he'd been startled out of a nap but Margo was busy texting, seemingly oblivious to what was going on.

It was suddenly important to Ian that he win Margo's attention. She was bone thin and braless in a retro tie-dyed T-shirt, torn jeans, and flip-flops. She wasn't his type at all, not that he'd turn her down if she threw herself at him, but she was a barometer of sorts. She was being paid to show an interest in him and if she was bored, it didn't say much for how his performance was going over with the people who weren't getting paid to be there.

Ian went on with his story, which he'd told a thousand times before. It usually got him big laughs and lots of sympathy.

"I was writing for a shrub with a badge. It was soul crushing. So I escaped into the action-packed world of Clint Straker and before I knew it, I had a novel. I sold the book, left the show, and my publishing career took off."

Book money wasn't quite as good as TV money but he was a single guy without much overhead, especially now that his house was in ashes and he liked being in control of his own creative life. He didn't have to write anything he didn't want to anymore and that was worth a slight drop in his income. The only things he didn't like about being an author instead of a TV writer were writing alone and buying his own lunch.

A frizzy-haired woman in the audience, dressed in a halter top that looked like it was hand-woven out of hemp, raised her hand. "How did you break your arm?"

"I wish I could say that I did it doing something heroic, like grabbing a suicidal woman just as she leaped off a freeway overpass and holding on to her until the fire department showed up," Ian said. "But the truth is that I fell off my bike. That's what I get for removing the training wheels."

He could tell from the expression on the woman's face that she wasn't amused. In fact, she seemed disappointed in him.

"You really aren't Clint Straker," she said.

"Nobody is."

Margo looked up at his remark and she seemed to like it. That pleased him until he realized how pathetic it was that he wanted her attention or her approval. He figured it only proved that no matter how successful he was—and he was, by just about any measure—he would always be just another insecure writer.

Ian signed books for the eight customers and left the bookstore with Margo five minutes later. Ordinarily, he would have stayed to autograph every book, on the off chance someone might buy a copy later. But he was right-handed and it wasn't easy signing with his arm in a cast, and the manager didn't ask him to, which wasn't very encouraging.

Margo drove Ian back to his downtown hotel in a rented Impala that felt ridiculously huge for only the two of them. It also seemed like the wrong car for her. She struck him as a VW Beetle kind of woman. Or maybe a Mini Cooper if she had some money, which she obviously didn't or the publisher would have reimbursed her gas and miles to drive him around Seattle rather than step up for a rental car. Maybe she didn't even own a car.

"That was disappointing," Ian said. "I usually draw a bigger crowd."

"It wasn't your fault," Margo said. "Union Bay is more of a literary bookstore."

"My books aren't literary?"

"They're spy novels," she said.

"That doesn't mean they aren't literary fiction. Somerset Maugham, Joseph Conrad, John le Carré, and Graham Greene all wrote spy novels."

"In your last book, Clint Straker seduced a female enemy agent and gave her an orgasm so intense that she fell into a coma for three days."

"He felt it was a more humane way of sidelining her than assassination," Ian said. "I think that shows his literary depth of character."

"It certainly does," she said.

He wasn't sure how to take that but he was pleased that she'd read the book and remembered the sex scene. And then he felt foolish that he felt that way. Something about her had turned him into an awkward teenager. It was probably because he hadn't been laid in ages and being around any woman made him stupidly eager to create a positive impression.

Margo pulled up to the entrance of the Sheraton Hotel at the corner of Sixth Avenue and Pike Street and parked the car outside the door.

"I'll meet you here at ten a.m. tomorrow for your signing at the Crime of Your Life bookstore," she said. "Do you want to keep the car for the rest of the day?"

"No, no, you take it. I think I'll stay in and write, maybe enjoy the room service—unless you'd like to join me."

Margo gave him a hard look. "I'm not that kind of escort."

Ian felt his face flush with embarrassment. "I wasn't suggesting—I mean, I wasn't implying that we'd be in my room. What I meant was that I'd eat with you somewhere that's not in my room if you wanted to eat, too."

She smiled, amused by his discomfort. "I was joking. I appreciate the invite but I've got dogs to walk and they're probably ready to burst."

"We wouldn't want that," Ian said, reaching across himself with his left hand to open his door. "Thanks for taking me around today. See you tomorrow."

He slid out of the seat, closed the door with his hip, and watched her drive off. Was it really an innocent misunderstanding or was he suggesting she come up to his room? He wasn't entirely sure. Maybe his desperation was coming through. With that in mind, he walked into the lobby and headed straight for the bar to see if there were any women around who'd jump at the chance to sleep with a *New York Times* bestselling author. But as he neared the bar, he could feel tension in the air like an electrical charge. Dozens of people were standing and staring at the wall-mounted TVs, all of which were tuned to CNN. The screens were filled with apocalyptic images of destruction in Waikiki and scores of injured people on the beach. Ian stopped just outside the bar and caught a portion of anchorman Wolf Blitzer's report.

> **BLITZER:** Thousands are hurt, hundreds are feared dead. Nobody knows at this point if the crash of TransAmerican 976 was the result of mechanical failure, human error, or an intentional act. But the parallels to 9/11 are impossible to ignore and deeply disturbing.

Ian shook his head and backed away from the bar, gripped by the crazy fear that someone might whirl around, recognize him, and shriek at the top of their lungs:

"You're responsible for this!"

CHAPTER THREE

Capitol Hill, Washington, DC. July 17. 6:00 p.m. Eastern Standard Time.

The hearing in the Senate chamber wasn't on any official schedule and began while TransAmerican 976 was boarding. There were no observers or reporters present. There wasn't even a stenographer. There were only the seven senators of the Intelligence Committee at the rostrum and the one man sitting at the witness table in front of them. The man's name was Wilton Cross. His bushy mustache, round cheeks, and double chin made him look lovable, like he'd be more comfortable as a department store Santa, or reading Dr. Seuss to his adorable grandchildren, than sitting in a bespoke $6,000 Italian suit, briefing politicians.

"For thirty years, I managed the CIA's covert operations on a day-to-day basis," Cross said. "In other words, I oversaw all of our surveillance, theft, sabotage, blackmail, smuggling, abduction, and killing."

The committee chairman—the corpulent, onetime-failed presidential nominee, Senator Ramsey Holbrook—harrumphed with disapproval. "I wouldn't characterize our intelligence efforts that way."

"That's one reason why the government shouldn't be doing this kind of work, Mr. Chairman," Cross said. "You can't do something well if you're in denial about what you're doing. Add to that the bureau-cracy, the limited budgets, the dated technology, and the fear of pros-ecution and what do you get? Fifty years of catastrophic intelligence failures. Meanwhile, the private sector, freed of those constraints, excels at the same work."

"Theft. Extortion. Kidnapping. Murder," said Senator Sam Tolan, a colorful Texas lawyer who enjoyed Stetson hats, Dallas Cowboys cheerleaders, and fat cigars, preferably all at once.

"That's right," Cross said.

Holbrook harrumphed again and browsed through the thick binder of material from Cross that each senator had in front of him.

"What you're proposing, Mr. Cross, is that we outsource our covert operations to you, Blackthorn Global Security. That's an auda-cious proposal, to say the least."

"But not unprecedented or unproven," Cross said. "We've had a long and successful outsourcing relationship with the Pentagon, fight-ing in places the military isn't authorized to be or engaging in activities they are prohibited from doing."

Senator Bradley Hazeltine, a fifth-generation politician from North Carolina, nodded. He'd emerged unscathed from three separate Justice Department corruption probes during his three terms in office, despite his guilt. "I must admit that those of us in intelligence oversight have been envious of the 'flexibility' enjoyed by our colleagues on the Armed Services Committee."

Envy was good. Cross could work with that. He continued his presentation, shifting his gaze from one senator to another as he spoke.

"Over the last decade, the nature of the threat to America has radi-cally changed. It's about terrorism now. Terrorists are swifter, more agile, and deadlier than armies. Borders are meaningless. Laws, ethics, morality, and accountability don't exist. We aren't on the same battle-field. We need to be or we're finished. Blackthorn will bring the war to them—only with greater technology and precision than our enemies."

"But with the same total disregard for legality, morality, and responsibility." That remark came from Kelly Stowe, the California senator with the perfect tan and capped teeth who'd turned to politics after his acting career fizzled out. Stowe took a lot of flak for frequently saying *dude* in his speeches from the Senate floor.

"Of course not, Senator," Cross said. "We'll go much further than that."

Stowe stared at him. "You can't be serious."

"Blackthorn will do whatever is necessary to protect our democracy."

"What you're describing is the antithesis of democracy," Stowe said.

"Not if you want it to survive," Cross said.

The room filled with a loud buzzing, as if a swarm of killer bees had suddenly invaded the chamber. It was the sound of every senator's smartphone vibrating at once. A mass alert couldn't be good news. The senators all reached for their devices and looked apprehensively at their screens.

The color couldn't have drained faster from Senator Holbrook's face if his throat had been slit. That was a fact, by the way, that Wilton Cross knew from personal experience.

"Oh my God," Holbrook said, rising with difficulty from his seat due to the emotional strain and his enormous weight. "We have an emergency. We need to adjourn and reconvene at another time."

"Of course," Cross said.

The senators quickly filed out through the door behind the rostrum without bothering to give Cross any details about the emergency. He didn't mind the slight. Cross was a spymaster. It was his job to already know what others knew. And he did this time, too.

He knew before it even happened.

CHAPTER FOUR

A floor-to-ceiling screen dominated the two-story, curved front wall in Blackthorn's situation room. The media wall showed a collage of feeds from all of the US television news broadcasts and video, both live and recorded, collected from a multitude of surveillance cameras in Waikiki as well as photos and videos of the plane crash and its catastrophic aftermath captured from social media sites. The screen depicted so much activity, drama, and emotion that it radiated a frenetic, psychic energy that was contagious, jacking up the anxiety level of every Blackthorn operative in the room.

There were two dozen workstations angled toward the media wall. The workstations were dominated by large ultrathin touch screens where the Blackthorn operatives manipulated data and video windows like mah-jongg tiles that could be sent to a colleague's screen or thrown up onto the media wall with a finger swipe.

Wilton Cross stood at the command console in the back of the room and watched the data gathering that his people were doing. He hit a button on his touch screen and Fox News anchor Shepard Smith took the center position on the media wall.

> **SMITH:** The president has been briefed and is monitoring the situation. A White House spokesman says at this point there is no evidence to suggest that this is a terrorist act.

"There isn't?" Cross posed the question to the room and hit a button on the console, muting the newscast. "Tell me what intel authorities have so far."

The first person to respond was Victoria Takahara, the analyst who sat to his left. She was a Pentagon hire who had spent most of her ten-year military career at a keyboard, directing drone strikes against terrorists. She'd killed more people from the comfort of a Herman Miller chair, with a Starbucks Cinnamon Dolce Latte in one hand, than most soldiers ever did on a battlefield. But Cross knew from reading the intelligence reports on her that in her private life she liked a more visceral experience, one that would make Christian Grey or the Marquis de Sade cower.

"The NTSB, FBI, Pentagon, and CIA have radar and satellite data that shows the plane prematurely leveled off after departure and turned east," Victoria said. "They also have audio of the pilot reporting an emergency and that they'd lost control of the aircraft."

"There's more." This time it was Seth Barclay who spoke. The former CIA analyst sat at Cross' right. His psychiatric profile described him as a highly functioning nonviolent sociopath afflicted with a hint of Asperger syndrome. He was thirty years old and his most intimate physical relationship to date was with his touch screen. "The authorities have the system data stream that's automatically transmitted by the plane to the airline and the engine manufacturer. The data indicates that the plane's autopilot was engaged and there were no mechanical malfunctions."

"How could the pilots have lost control if the autopilot was on and there were no malfunctions?" Cross said. "Who is asking those questions?"

"Probably everybody involved in the investigation," Seth said.

Cross pointed to the news broadcasts streaming on the media wall. "I mean out there."

"No one yet," Seth said. "The media doesn't have the data."

"Change that. Leak the information we have to some of the aviation pundits under contract to the TV networks," Cross said. "Encourage them to start speculating on the worst possible scenarios."

"They won't need the encouragement," Victoria said. "Fear is what keeps them on the air and getting paid."

"What about background on the passengers and crew?" Cross asked. "Any red flags that we can exploit, like felony criminal records, terrorist ties, diagnosed mental instability?"

"None so far," Victoria said. "But I doubt it was a flight full of angels."

"If they weren't before," Seth said, "they are now."

"I'm sure there are a few who are on a spit and getting stabbed with a pitchfork," Victoria said.

Cross knew that she might as well be describing her idea of casual foreplay. "I want updates every fifteen minutes."

"Yes, sir," she said.

Cross walked out of the situation room and headed down the hallway, past several conference rooms, to his large corner office, which had an adjoining private apartment as luxuriously appointed as a suite at the Four Seasons. It sure beat the vinyl-upholstered couch and minifridge that he'd had in his cramped basement office at the CIA. He'd spent many nights on that damn couch. Now when work demanded that he spend the night in the office, he enjoyed a king-size bed fitted with sumptuous 1,020-thread-count sheets of Egyptian cotton, gossamer-woven in Italy by naked nubile virgins.

The part about the nubile virgins was just a guess on his part. But the thought of it often eased him into a peaceful sleep with a languid hard-on.

CHAPTER FIVE

Sheraton Hotel, Seattle, Washington. July 18. 3:47 a.m. Pacific Standard Time.

The only light in Ian Ludlow's dark hotel room came from the open, ravaged minibar and the flickering glow from the TV, which had been playing CNN all night. Jake Tapper was on the air now, giving an update against a backdrop of photos of the devastation in Honolulu. It looked like nuclear winter had come to paradise. A ticker-tape crawl at the bottom of the screen kept a gruesome tally of the victims like the score of a football game. Two hundred thirty-eight people were dead, 117 injured, but both numbers were expected to rise.

> **TAPPER:** At the same moment air traffic controllers noticed that the plane had changed its heading and leveled off, the pilots radioed the tower that they'd lost control of the aircraft. With me now is Shawn Danielson, a former NTSB investigator and our senior aviation editor. Shawn, what does that tell you?

Danielson was a talking head in his fifties with dark circles under his hangdog eyes. He was wearing a wrinkled Lacoste polo shirt that looked as if it might have been yanked out of the hamper. He joined Tapper on Skype from what appeared to be his kitchen table. Danielson's backdrop was a toaster oven and microwave on a granite countertop.

> **DANIELSON:** A horrifying story, Jake. All departing aircraft leaving Honolulu International immediately turn away from Waikiki toward the open sea to avoid flying low over the beaches. But 976 didn't do that. The plane leveled off at twelve hundred feet, then veered toward the beach in a fast, steady descent. In fact, I've learned from sources close to the investigation that data transmitted during takeoff indicates that the autopilot was engaged.

> **TAPPER:** Are you saying that the crash was deliberate?

> **DANIELSON:** There is no other explanation.

Ian was lying fully dressed on top of the bed, his back propped up with pillows, staring at the TV. Empty mini-bottles from the minibar were scattered on the bed, along with candy bar wrappers and crinkled empty bags of chips. He chewed on the last bite of his last Toblerone and wondered for perhaps the hundredth time if he was having a waking nightmare or if this was really happening.

Maybe it was all just a horrible coincidence.

Maybe he had nothing to do with it.

Then again, maybe he did.

Maybe it all began three years ago with a group of writers gathered in a mountain cabin, making up stories. He hadn't seen the harm in it. It was all make-believe. A story never killed anyone.

Until now.

CHAPTER SIX

Somewhere in Maine. Three Years Ago. Winter.

"What about a plane crash?" Ian said.

The six men were gathered in a remote log cabin in the middle of a snowy forest. The interior was almost entirely decorated in animal hides and wood. The sofa and armchairs were upholstered in leather, the rugs were cowhide, and the tables were rough-hewn antique walnut. A roaring fire crackled in a big fieldstone hearth and a pair of moose antlers was mounted over the log mantel. Ian half expected Daniel Boone to bound in, shake the snow off his bearskin jacket, and toss his coonskin cap on one of those antlers.

Ian sat in an armchair that was as close to the fire as he could get without setting his cable-knit wool sweater aflame. He was from Southern California so his idea of a freezing temperature was anything below sixty degrees and it was a good thirty degrees below that outside. Just looking at the frosty windows made him shiver.

"A plane crash has been done," said Clayton Roper, a heavyset man in his sixties who sat in the armchair beside Ian and sucked on his pipe like it was his only source of oxygen. "Nine/eleven, the shoe bomber, that suicidal pilot who flew into a mountain. It's become a cliché. I thought we're supposed to be using our imaginations. How about smallpox?"

"What about it?" asked Kurt Delmore, a screenwriter who sat on one end of the sofa, absently stroking his graying hipster goatee. He was a forty-year-old man with the beginnings of a beer belly under his vintage bowling shirt.

"It's a virus that has killed millions over the centuries. Nobody is vaccinated against smallpox anymore because everybody thinks it has been eradicated. But in reality, it hasn't been," Clayton said. "There are vials of the stuff out there, weaponized and jacked up with Ebola and other nightmarish shit. What if terrorists get hold of a vial? What if they get vaccinated, then go to the Super Bowl and use pocket atomizers, disguised as breath fresheners or inhalers for people with asthma, and spritz the virus into the crowd? Thousands of people would be infected in seconds without even knowing it. In ten days, an epidemic could spread across the nation, if not the world, creating a global pandemic that could wipe out three-quarters of humanity."

"That sounds like one of your Deathfist novels to me," Kurt said.

"It is," Clayton said. "That's how I know the plot works."

"We aren't here to reuse our old plots but to think up new ones," Kurt said. "Here's a fun fact: Los Angeles uses an underground cavern to store enough natural gas to heat the city for a year. The cavern is located behind thousands of homes. What if terrorists ignited the gas? The massive explosion would make the Big One seem like a fart."

"I'm not sure your science is right," said Jose Contreras from where he sat at the kitchen table, hunched over a sketch pad, smoking a joint, and drawing a picture of a runaway train going off the rails in a fiery blast. He was the youngest man in the room by at least a decade, and was a renowned author and illustrator of graphic novels. "Maybe the gas wouldn't explode and instead you'd create a geyser of fire that couldn't be put out."

"That's cool," Kurt said.

"Yeah, but it wouldn't be a catastrophe," Jose said. "It might become a tourist attraction instead. But I know for a fact that a runaway train full of crude oil derailed in Canada and the inferno decimated an entire town. We could work with that."

He held up his sketch for everyone to see. It looked to Ian like a freeze-frame from an action-movie sequence, as if all it would take was someone hitting play on a remote for the catastrophe to unfold on the page. Jose had talent, but Ian wasn't wild about the derailed train idea.

"Getting back to the plane crash," Ian said. "I understand your objections, Clayton, but I'm not talking about a hijacking or a bomb. I'm talking about using planes as guided missiles."

"Forgetting for a moment how boring and familiar that is," Clayton said, "there's intense levels of security now at airports and in planes strictly to prevent that scenario from happening. You know why? Because what you're talking about has already been done. Move on."

But Ian wasn't giving up yet. "What if I could crash a plane into downtown San Francisco, or the Las Vegas Strip, or anyplace I want, anytime I want, without setting foot in the airport or on the aircraft?"

"Are you just throwing the notion out there for discussion?" That question came from Bob, the man who'd brought them all here. It was the first time he'd spoken in two hours.

Bob sat on the couch on the opposite corner from Kurt. There was something grandfatherly and comforting about Bob, unlike the stony-faced man who stood at the wall near the front door, his arms crossed under his chest, wearing an earpiece that kept him in contact with the other stony-faced men who were somewhere outside in the snow.

"Or do you have a way to do it?" Bob added.

"I think I do," Ian said. "You'll have to find out if it's actually possible. But isn't that why the CIA invited us out here?"

Bob smiled. "Tell us your evil plan."

CHAPTER SEVEN

Sheraton Hotel, Seattle, Washington. July 18. 3:48 a.m. Pacific Standard Time.

Ian reached for the iPhone on his nightstand and called Clayton Roper, who lived on Cape Cod, where he'd churned out a book a month in his Deathfist series for decades. The books were about Michel Sang, an ex-priest turned assassin and restaurateur who was an expert in all of the martial, erotic, and culinary arts. It was one of the last surviving series in the men's action-adventure genre that once included heroes like the Executioner, the Penetrator, the Destroyer, the S.O.B.s, Black Samurai, and Mr. Jury.

The phone was answered by a young woman on the second ring. "Hello. This is Emily."

Ian sat up straighter in bed and tried to quash his anxiety from creeping into his voice. "Good morning, Emily. My name is Ian Ludlow. I'm sorry to be calling so early but I have to speak to Clayton."

"That's not going to happen."

"It's urgent. I'm sure that he won't mind if you wake him up for this."

"I wish I could," Emily said. "But I don't have the power to raise the dead."

Her last word hit Ian like a bucket of ice water poured over his head. He was stunned and yet completely alert. "Did you say . . . dead?"

"My father died six weeks ago," she said, a weariness creeping into her voice, "so you can forget about whatever he owes you."

"I'm not after any money. I was a friend of his. I'm a writer, too. I write the Clint Straker novels."

"Forgive me, I don't read much and I didn't mean to be rude. I'm his only child, and ever since he died, I've been getting calls from bill collectors. I had no idea he was having any financial trouble so that's been a shock, too. Dad never talked to me about that kind of thing."

"It's okay, I totally understand. I can only imagine how overwhelming it must be for you to have to deal with all of this," Ian said. "If you don't mind, may I ask how he died?"

"He was out fishing and his boat capsized. He drowned."

For a moment, Ian couldn't summon the air to breathe, much less speak. The implications of what she said were too horrifying to consider and they put recent events in his own life in a whole new light.

"Were you two close?" Emily asked.

"No, not really," Ian replied, almost in a whisper. He cleared his throat and regained his voice. "We met at a writers' conference a few years ago. He had a vivid imagination."

"It sustained him, financially and in just about every other way, but I guess that's true of most writers. He was always emotionally distant. Sometimes it felt like he was saving his emotional investments for the characters in his books. He definitely cared more about Michel Sang, the Deathfist, than he did any of his wives," Emily said. "Forgive me again, I'm rambling. What was the urgent matter you needed to discuss with him?"

"It's irrelevant now," Ian said. "I'm sorry for your loss."

Ian ended the call, tossed the phone on the bed, then reached down with his good arm to pick up his MacBook from the floor. He set the computer on his lap, raised the screen to wake it from its snooze, and typed "Kurt Delmore" with his left hand into the search window of his browser. In an instant, the Google search results came up on his screen, arranged by date. The most recent mention was an article from Deadline Hollywood, the entertainment industry news site.

It was Kurt Delmore's obituary.

CHAPTER EIGHT

Blackthorn Global Security Headquarters, Bethesda, Maryland. July 18. 7:10 a.m. Eastern Standard Time.

Victoria Takahara was at her touch screen, scrolling through the petty criminal record of a TransAmerican 976 passenger, when she heard an alert beep from her computer. A telephone icon blinked on her screen. She tapped it. A graphic of an audio recording that resembled an EKG readout popped up with two phone numbers listed underneath it. One number was Ian Ludlow's iPhone. The other was Clayton Roper's home phone in Cape Cod. Both devices were constantly monitored by Blackthorn and all calls, sent or received, were automatically recorded, flagged, and archived. The time stamp showed that the call had occurred only moments ago. She touched the app's play button and listened.

EMILY: Hello. This is Emily.

IAN: Good morning, Emily. My name is Ian Ludlow. I'm sorry to be calling so early but I have to speak to Clayton.

EMILY: That's not going to happen.

IAN: It's urgent—

Victoria swore to herself, tapped the screen to pause the recording, and then typed a command on her keyboard.

An instant later Ian Ludlow's worried face appeared in a window on her screen as if they were having a live FaceTime video chat. In a sense they were, only it was one-way. He didn't know that his camera was on. The green light on the top edge of his screen that would ordinarily have lit up when his camera was on had been deactivated by Victoria's hacking program the instant she'd hijacked his MacBook to spy on him. His microphone was live, too, recording the sound of his anxious breathing. The hacking program was also recording his keystrokes, capturing his passwords and anything else he wrote.

She tapped on Ian's face with her cursor and a new window opened in front of her, showing her exactly what he was looking at on his MacBook screen. He'd pulled up the month-old Deadline Hollywood obituary for Kurt Delmore, a screenwriter of low-budget action movies who'd died of a heart attack in his sleep.

She looked at Ian. His face betrayed his shock and increasing horror at what he was learning from the information on-screen. This wasn't good for either of them.

Victoria picked up her phone and called Cross at his office. He answered immediately, awake and alert.

"Cross."

"Sir, we have a problem developing."

"What is it?"

"Ian Ludlow called Clayton Roper. Now he's checking out the others."

He hung up without a word. She set the phone down in its cradle and a moment later Cross marched into the situation room.

"Show me," he said.

Victoria swiped both of the windows up on her touch screen and they disappeared from her monitor and appeared in the center of the media wall as if they'd flown there from her desk. Now everyone in the situation room could see that Ian Ludlow was googling another name: Jose Contreras.

"He's connecting the dots," Cross said.

Several search results came up on Ian's MacBook. The top one was a *Los Angeles Times* article from a few weeks ago reporting on the graphic artist's tragic death from a drug overdose.

Ian Ludlow is the luckiest man on earth, Cross thought. They'd made two attempts to kill him already, both designed to look like accidents, but he'd survived. Cross decided at the time that making a third within weeks of the other two might appear suspicious to local authorities and might prompt an investigation. Now he wished he'd taken the gamble.

Everyone in the situation room watched as Ian pulled up the *Los Angeles Times* article and scrolled through it, stopping at the paragraph that described Jose as a recovering drug addict and expressed his family's shock that he'd fallen prey to demons that they thought he'd conquered years ago.

Ian looked at the cast on his right arm. Cross saw the dawning realization, and the accompanying horror, in the naked, completely unguarded expression on Ian's face. The writer knew he was a dead man. He slammed the laptop closed and both of the surveillance windows on the media wall went dark.

Cross turned to Seth. "Where is Ludlow now?"

"He's in Seattle at the Sheraton Hotel on Sixth and Pike. Room 3016. He's on a book tour for his new novel." Seth swiped up onto the media wall a screen grab of Ian's book tour itinerary from his publisher's website. "He's signing at the Crime of Your Life bookstore at ten thirty this morning and then he goes to Denver this afternoon."

Cross turned to Victoria. "Where's our nearest asset?"

"Waiting for him in Denver," Victoria said. "She can be in Seattle in three hours."

"That's not soon enough," Cross said, then raised his voice so everyone in the situation room could hear him. "Listen up. This is a priority-one alert. I want eyes and ears on Ludlow at all times. Full Big Brother. Starting now. We need to take this player off the board."

Ian sat on his hotel room toilet, his pants bunched up around his feet, crapping his guts out in sheer terror. He'd felt his sphincters opening up the instant he'd closed his laptop and had barely made it to the bathroom in time.

He'd dreamed up a terrorist plot to kill hundreds of people as a hypothetical scenario for the CIA so they could prevent it from ever happening. Instead the CIA used his idea to attack their own country for some twisted reason he couldn't imagine. Or maybe he could, given enough time. He was a writer and imagining was his job. But time was something he didn't have . . . because the CIA was out to kill him.

Hell, maybe he deserved to die. Hundreds of people were dead in Hawaii. He didn't crash that plane himself but it was his fucking idea. He was the author of all that destruction.

He felt his bowels blow again but he was empty inside. Instead his purged intestines tangled themselves up in knots of fear that made him curl up with pain. He hugged himself and rocked on the toilet. It was little comfort.

How was he going to survive? And how would he live with himself if he did?

CHAPTER NINE

Ian peeked out from behind a pillar outside the Sheraton's lobby and saw Margo walking from the street toward the automatic doors. She wore a black tank top, pre-torn jeans, and ankle boots. He stepped out of hiding just as she passed.

"Margo. Over here."

She jerked, startled, her hand reflexively going to her chest. He wondered why people, particularly women, touched their chests when they were surprised. He made a mental note to ask an expert in human nature to explain it to him. It would make a cool fact for his next book, assuming he lived long enough to write another one.

"Sorry," he said. "I didn't mean to scare you."

Margo cocked her head and studied him. He had his leather messenger bag over his right shoulder and his Samsonite rolling carry-on suitcase at his left side. He was wearing the same wrinkled clothes from the previous day, his cast was spattered with melted chocolate, and he was looking around furtively with bloodshot eyes.

"Were you hiding?" she asked.

Yes, and it was stupid, because he knew it was no secret that he was in Seattle or even that he was staying at the Sheraton. He'd sent a tweet to his 5,788 followers when he'd landed and posted photos on Instagram of the welcome basket full of local fruits, cookies, and candies that was waiting for him in his room. Perhaps hiding was what people instinctively did when they felt threatened, even if it made no logical sense. He'd have to ask the human nature expert about that, too.

"No, of course not," he said. "That would be stupid. Where did you park the car?"

"In the hotel garage. I figured we'd walk to the bookstore. It's only a few blocks away."

"Good thinking. Rental cars are equipped with GPS transponders so they can be constantly tracked by the rental companies."

That was a cool fact he'd picked up while researching one of his Clint Straker books. Now it might help save him in real life.

"That's nice to know," Margo said. "But I think I'll remember where I parked without having to call Hertz for help."

Ian looked around, trying to decide where to go next. The Sheraton was on a hill. He could go uphill on Pike Street, east toward the freeway and Lake Washington, or head downhill, west toward the iconic Pike Place Market and the waters of Elliott Bay. He could take a ferry from there to someplace. But where? Or he could go northwest on Sixth Avenue, taking him downhill toward the Space Needle. He wasn't going up there. That was a mistake people always made in books and movies. They headed up only to fall a long way down.

His remaining option was heading south on Sixth, down toward Pioneer Square. Something drew him in that direction. Perhaps it was instinct again, pulling him toward Los Angeles, his home, hundreds of miles south. He started walking fast down the street, rolling his suitcase along with him.

"Wait a minute," Margo said, hurrying after him. "Your flight to Denver isn't until four. We can leave your bags here and come back for them after the signing."

"I'm not going to the signing and I'm sure as hell not coming back here." He also had no intention of going to Denver or anywhere else on his itinerary. It was bad enough that they knew he was in Seattle.

Margo was confused. "Then where are we going?"

"Is your phone on?"

"Yes."

"Turn it off. They can track that, too."

"Who?" she asked.

"The people who are trying to kill me."

Those people were watching Ian and Margo on the media wall in Blackthorn's situation room. The huge screen showed the two of them from different angles culled from an array of cameras in the area: building security cameras, ATM cameras, traffic cameras, and even the cell phone cameras of people taking selfies and sightseeing photos and then posting them to social media.

"They are heading west on Sixth Avenue," Seth said.

Cross nodded. "How many parked vehicles can we access within a four-block radius of their location?"

Seth typed a few keys. A satellite view of the downtown Seattle streets showed up on the media wall. Lots of red dots, each representing a parked car that could be remotely hacked, blinked along the streets and within parking structures.

"Forty-six," Seth said. "Of those, twenty-one have ignitions that can be started through the manufacturer's smartphone app. Fourteen of those cars have parking assist and five have full autopilot capability."

Cross smiled. "Find me one with autopilot that's parked on a steep hill."

CHAPTER TEN

Ian and Margo were on Sixth Avenue and crossing against the light at the intersection with University Street. Ian had no idea where he was going. All he knew was that he couldn't stay where he was. So his only plan at the moment was to keep moving and not to be a sitting target.

"Nobody wants to kill you," Margo said.

"You haven't turned off your phone."

Margo reached into her pocket, pulled out her iPhone, and made a show of turning it off. "Satisfied?"

"You think I'm crazy."

"I think you're paranoid from drugs, drinking, and sleep deprivation," she said. "We've all been there."

"I didn't take any drugs," Ian said, walking fast.

"But you drank everything in the minibar," she said. "I can smell it."

"I was trying to numb the terror." It was a lie. The terror came after the crushing guilt—that's what he was really trying to numb but he wasn't ready to tell her about that yet. He was barely ready to admit it to himself. "You would have done the same thing after what I've been through."

"I was with you all day yesterday," Margo said. "The closest you came to getting killed was when you made a pass at me."

"The attempt on my life didn't happen yesterday. Two months ago, one of the burners on my stove was left on. I didn't smell the gas because my allergies were really bad so I took a bath to clear my sinuses and relax," Ian said. "I was in the bathtub at the other end of the house when the place exploded. The stuffy nose saved my life. They didn't anticipate that."

"They?" Margo asked. "Who are they?"

They were carefully tracking Ian and Margo on the media wall.

"There's a loaded Mercedes S-Class with autopilot parked on Madison above the intersection with Sixth Avenue," Seth said. "If Ludlow keeps walking south, he'll cross the intersection."

"Let's see the car," Cross said.

Several windows opened up on the media wall, each showing a different security-camera view of a black Mercedes sedan facing downhill on a very steep street.

Cross glanced at Victoria. "Do you have access?"

"I do."

Victoria hit a button on her keyboard and started the car's ignition.

Ian and Margo approached Sixth Avenue. The light was red. A half block uphill, a black Mercedes rolled away from the curb. Without a driver. But they didn't see that.

"They tried again three weeks ago," Ian said, stopping at the corner. "I was riding my bike on Mulholland, up in the Santa Monica Mountains. I do that every weekend. I was going too fast. I tried to slow down but my brakes failed. I swerved into traffic, got clipped by a car, and went flying off a cliff. I smacked into a rock outcropping on my way down. It broke my fall and my arm; otherwise I'd be dead. Now I know my bike was sabotaged and the car hit me on purpose."

"You're just having a run of bad luck."

"They are. I'm not. I'm on a winning streak. I'm still alive. But they will try again. They have to."

The light turned green and Ian bounded into the street, rolling his suitcase behind him. Ian was centered in the Mercedes' hood ornament like it was a gunsight. He didn't see the black car speeding down the hill straight for him.

But Margo did.

She dashed into the intersection and took a flying leap that would have made Clint Straker proud, tackling Ian and taking them both down, the two of them barely clearing the car's shiny grille. They hit the ground hard. The Mercedes smashed into Ian's suitcase, splitting it open in a spray of clothes.

The Mercedes roared past Ian and Margo. They both looked up to get a glimpse through the flying underwear and socks at the insane son of a bitch driving the car.

But there was nobody in the driver's seat.

They were still absorbing that chilling fact when the car blasted into the intersection and was T-boned by a bus.

The bus bulldozed the Mercedes down Sixth Avenue in a shower of sparks, broken glass, and ripped sheet metal and plowed it into the row of cars ahead, causing a chain reaction of rear-end collisions that stretched half a block.

Ian propped himself up on his good elbow and stared down at the intersection. It looked like the aftermath of a monster truck derby. People on the sidewalks, and from within the surrounding businesses, rushed into the street to help the injured and the trapped.

"There was nobody driving the car," Ian said.

He felt oddly calm and it came through in the matter-of-fact way he shared his observation with Margo.

He'd felt a different kind of calm when he'd sat up naked in his bathtub, his hair singed, and realized that most of his house was gone. That calm was shock, the mental numbness that comes from experiencing a traumatic event. This calm was certainty, the intellectual peace that comes from achieving clarity and understanding. The CIA was definitely trying to kill him. But how did they know he would be crossing that street at that moment?

"It's a steep hill." Margo sat up, dazed and sore. "The parking brake failed. It happens."

"Uh-huh," Ian said. "Then why was the engine running?"

"Because some dipshit left his car double-parked with the engine running while he ran into a building to do some dipshit errand," Margo said. "He deserves to lose his fucking hundred-thousand-dollar car."

"If the car was idling at the curb when the brake failed," Ian said, "why was it rolling straight down the center of the street?"

It wouldn't be. Someone had to turn the wheel and keep it steady.

Ian was right and Margo knew it. But he didn't see her eyes widen in fear as she accepted his argument. His gaze was fixed on the office building across the street and the array of security cameras out front that were aimed in their general direction.

CHAPTER ELEVEN

Ian Ludlow's face on the media wall was like an angry giant peering down at the Blackthorn operatives through a window. He knew they were there, watching him, even if he couldn't actually see them. Every operative was waiting to see how Cross would react to the failed operation.

But Cross was thinking about the Rogue Element, the one complication, behavior, object, or occurrence in any operation that couldn't be anticipated, regardless of whether a mission was simple or complex, improvised or carefully planned.

Because Cross was exceptionally good at his job, more often than not the Rogue Element ended up being only a minor annoyance. Sometimes it was even a source of amusement, easing the tension of a deadly operation. But it could also lead to devastating failure and many lost lives.

The rock outcropping, the bathtub, and now a woman were the Rogue Elements that had saved Ian Ludlow from a premeditated accidental death. Those failures were embarrassing but the fate of the larger operation wasn't jeopardized yet. They still had time to clean up their mess. However, the risk to them increased with each passing hour that Ludlow still drew breath.

The key to overcoming the Rogue Element, whenever it appeared, was operational flexibility and a clear head. What Cross needed now were more facts before he could decide on a course of action. So, when he finally spoke, his voice was even and calm, betraying neither his anger nor his frustration.

"Who is that woman with Ludlow?"

Seth typed a command on his keyboard. One of the camera images of Margo on the media wall froze. Targeting points appeared on Margo's face as the facial recognition software analyzed her features against the millions of other faces in their database. Her driver's license, University of Washington student ID, credit card photos, and a blizzard of other bits and pieces of her life appeared on the big screen. Operatives around the situation room began shouting out details about her as they found them.

"Her name is Margo French."

"She's an author escort. Ludlow's publisher hired her to take him around town for his events."

"She's twenty-four years old, single, and a college dropout."

"She lives in a studio apartment in the university district."

"She used to work at the bookstore Ludlow visited last night."

"She owes two thousand seven hundred and fifty-eight dollars on her credit card, buys her groceries at Whole Foods, and her most recent Amazon purchase was a Lipstick Vibrator."

Cross asked the room, "Does she have any special skills?"

"She was a goalie on her high school soccer team in Walla Walla."

"She plays guitar and sings at local coffeehouses."

"She's got seventy-four positive reviews on Yelp for dog sitting."

Victoria said, "She's an easy kill."

"So is Ludlow and we've failed three times," Cross said.

Ian shrugged off his messenger bag, which had broken his fall, and got shakily to his feet, using his good, left arm to push himself up. Once he was standing, he didn't pick up his bag. He'd decided to ditch it and the computer inside. If he kept the MacBook, it would reveal his location to the CIA the instant it was turned on. He felt claustrophobic, even though he was out in the open. He could feel the world closing in on him.

"We have to get out of here," he said.

"Not me." Margo stood up and examined the scrapes on her arms. "I'm done with this crazy shit. I'm going home."

She started to walk back the way they came but Ian grabbed her arm.

"You can't go home," he said. "You're in danger."

"No, I'm not." Margo easily yanked her arm free from his weak grasp. "Whoever they are, they aren't after me."

"They are now. You see those cameras across the street? Do you see the ones behind us? Do you see the traffic cameras in the intersection? There are cameras everywhere and they can access them all," Ian said. "That's how they knew where I'd be so they could hack a car to run me down. They know that you saw it. They are watching us both right now. I'm sorry, but now you're in as much danger as I am."

She looked around at the cameras and thought about what he'd said. Ian knew what he was saying sounded like the rantings of a lunatic and yet he could see from the expression on her face that it was beginning to make sense to her. That's because his explanation was sensibly crazy: sensible in the context of what had just happened, but crazy if considered on its own. He'd used that argument in the writers' room to justify all kinds of stupid stuff on *Hollywood & the Vine* and in the privacy of his own office on plot points in his books.

"Who are they?" she demanded. "Why do they want to kill you?"

Ian heard sirens approaching. The police and fire departments would be here in minutes. They were running out of time. "I promise that I will tell you everything but right now we have to disappear or we're dead."

"Why can't we just wait for the police and ask for their protection?"

"Because they can't protect us. Nobody can. You have to trust me, at least until we're somewhere safe and I have the time to explain, or we're both going to be killed today."

She had the look on her face of a struggling math student trying to solve a difficult algebra problem in her head.

"Fuck you," she said. "Follow me."

Margo took off downhill and Ian followed her. They ran through the intersection, weaving through the cars and the pandemonium, down toward Fifth Avenue.

The camera feeds on the media wall tracked the pair's zigzagging flight on foot through the streets and alleys of downtown Seattle.

The situation room was still silent, although plenty of activity was going on. Half of the Blackthorn operatives present were working the covert op that was unfolding in Seattle. They were frantically accessing private and municipal cameras throughout the area to maintain visual surveillance on the two targets. They were also actively monitoring street and air traffic, police and fire department communications and deployment, and any other activities that could potentially impact the outcome of the op.

The remaining operatives were focused on the aftermath of the Honolulu plane crash: monitoring the FBI, Homeland Security, and NTSB investigations, tracking news and social media coverage, and doing background checks on all of the airplane passengers, flight crew, airport ground crew, and investigators working the case.

"Based on what we know about Ludlow and French," Cross said, "can we anticipate where they are headed?"

"Pioneer Square," Seth said.

"What's there that's significant to them?"

"The Crime of Your Life bookstore," Seth said. "They're late for Ludlow's signing."

CHAPTER TWELVE

Ian and Margo ran out of an alley onto Cherry Street, stopping to catch their breath on the sidewalk directly across from the Crime of Your Life bookstore, which was on the ground floor of an old office building. A poster-size blowup of Ian's book cover filled the window and a banner over the entrance read: **IAN LUDLOW SIGNING TODAY!**

"You can't be serious," Ian said. "This is the first place that they'll look for me."

"Follow my lead." She looked both ways for traffic, crossed the steep street, and waited for him at the door to the bookstore.

Ian hesitated but decided he had no choice. He dashed across the street and she held the door open for him.

The tiny bookstore was jammed with bookshelves from floor to ceiling. Even the checkout counter, where the store manager was stationed, was essentially a waist-high set of bookshelves. The store could barely hold the two dozen people, mostly middle-aged women, who stood in the three narrow aisles, clutching hardcover copies of *The Dead Never Forget*. He forced a smile and went inside.

The manager's name was Dottie, presumably for her galaxy of freckles and her affection for polka-dotted dresses, and the instant she saw Ian coming in she loudly declared, "Ian Ludlow is in the building."

And then Dottie led the customers in applause. Even Margo joined in.

"Sorry I'm late," Ian said. "I've been on the run all morning."

It was a line worthy of Clint Straker and Ian knew it. He couldn't stop being a writer, always thinking of the next line in one of his thrillers. But he was living a thriller now and it was no thrill at all.

Pictures of Ian Ludlow, taken by customers in the store and being posted to Twitter, Facebook, Instagram, and Pinterest, began showing up on the media wall almost immediately after his arrival. It was the only view Cross had of what was going on inside the bookstore, though he had multiple camera angles on the exterior.

"Why did he go there?" Cross wondered aloud.

"Maybe he thinks there's safety in a crowd," Seth said.

"Or maybe he can't pass up a chance to autograph his books," Victoria said.

Neither explanation satisfied Cross. He frowned and folded his arms under his chest. What was Ian Ludlow thinking?

Ludlow was certainly carrying a heavy emotional and psychological burden. He believed the CIA was responsible for the crash of TransAmerican 976, killing hundreds and wounding even more, and he knew that it began as his idea. That had to scare him. There was also the terror of knowing he was being watched and relentlessly pursued by killers. In fact, only moments ago he'd barely escaped being run down by a remote-controlled car.

So how did Ludlow react? He ran to a bookstore to autograph some books. Not just any random bookstore, but the one he was scheduled to be at right now, where killers could already be waiting or could show up any minute. Cross didn't have any killers in Seattle yet, but Ludlow didn't know that.

What Ludlow did was insane. Had he cracked?

Or was he seeking solace for his anguish, or distraction from his fear, in the adulation of his fans while he figured out what to do next? That was the sort of superficial, ego-driven thing an insecure writer might do.

Or perhaps he'd simply realized the futility of running, that he couldn't escape his fate. So Ludlow decided that he might as well enjoy the last moment of happiness he was likely to have in the short time he had left alive.

That explanation made some sense to Cross. It was a logical and rational reaction. And maybe if Ludlow had been alone in his flight, Cross could have accepted that as a working theory.

But there was still Margo French, the Rogue Element, to consider. She'd saved Ludlow's life and then run to the bookstore with him. He didn't believe that she did it because she was worried about them being late to his signing.

No, there had to be something more there, too.

What was she thinking? More important, what had Ludlow told her?

Nothing about this felt right. Cross was certain that he was missing a crucial piece of information.

"Bring up every camera you can access on the entire block," Cross said to his operatives. "Public or private, interior and exterior. Run it all through real-time facial recognition. If Ludlow and French show their faces, I want to see them."

"Ian's not feeling well," Margo confided to Dottie while Ian posed for selfies with some of the attendees. "May he use the bathroom?"

"Of course. You know where it is."

Margo moved away from the counter and took Ian gently by his good arm as she addressed the crowd. "Mr. Ludlow will be right back."

She led him through the crowd to a door in the back of the store. The door led into a cramped storeroom full of books and cleaning supplies.

"What are we doing here?" Ludlow asked.

"Disappearing."

"Everybody in the store knows we're here."

"Don't be an idiot," she said.

There were two more doors in the room. One door was ajar, revealing a cramped bathroom. She closed the bathroom door, went to the other door, slipped the bolt, and opened it, revealing a rickety set of wooden stairs descending into darkness.

"This way," Margo said. "Hold on to the railing as you go down. I don't want you breaking your neck before I get an explanation for everything."

He followed her down the stairs. As they neared the bottom, Ian's eyes adjusted to the darkness and he realized that diffused light was coming from somewhere. The air was musty from moisture and lack of circulation. It smelled like history. He made a mental note to remember that description.

Ian found himself in what appeared to be an alley between two buildings, which made no sense at all. He found it very disorienting. It didn't help that he was sleep deprived, hungover, and crashing from the adrenaline jolt of his near-death experience.

Margo led him out onto what appeared to be an underground street that was lined on both sides with dirt-caked, cobwebbed storefronts with bricked-up doors and windows. It was like the exterior set of a Western street from an old movie that had been rebuilt in someone's basement. The dim light that allowed him to see it all was coming from filthy glass-cubed skylights embedded in the sidewalk above their heads. The muddy ground was littered with beer bottles, soiled mattresses, and fast-food containers.

Here he was underground, with walls all around him, and yet his claustrophobia was gone. Here he felt free. Nobody could see him here.

"What is this place?" he asked.

"Old Seattle." She hurried through the underground maze and he struggled to keep up with her. It wasn't easy running with one arm in a cast in the best of circumstances, much less in half darkness over rutted dirt and patches of mud. "Pioneer Square is built on Puget Sound muck. It used to flood here all the time. So, in the late 1890s, the city began raising the streets."

"How did they do that?"

"They basically built bridges on top of the old streets. The second floor of every building became the new ground floor," she said. "But it didn't happen overnight. For a while, people still used these underground streets to get around and do business. That's why there're skylights in the sidewalks overhead. Some of the homeless come down here for the night and for shelter during the winter."

"How do you know so much about it?"

"It's not a big secret," she said. "There are tours of a few buried streets that've been 'restored' by repainting signage, scattering around some wooden barrels and wagon wheels, and adding a few dusty mannequins dressed in old-fashioned clothes. It's a rip-off that caters to morons."

But at least the air on those tour streets probably wasn't tinged with the lingering scents of stale beer and urine. The farther away they got from the bookstore, the more the underground smelled to Ian like a public bathroom on Santa Monica Beach. Even so, he'd never seen a place like this.

"This would be a cool location for a killing."

She gave him a look. "Isn't that what we're trying to avoid?"

"Good point," he said.

CHAPTER THIRTEEN

Cross scanned the images on the big-screen wall and realized that there weren't any new pictures from Ludlow's book-signing event posted on social media. "When was the last time a photo was posted of Ludlow?"

"Three minutes ago," Seth said.

That wasn't good. Cross' instincts were telling him something was wrong.

"Call the bookstore," Cross said to Victoria. "Tell them you're Ludlow's editor and you need to share some great news with him right away."

Victoria picked up the phone and made the call, introduced herself, and asked for Ian. Cross tuned out the one-sided phone conversation, his eyes scanning the camera feeds, looking for anything amiss. All he saw were the crowds of people in Pioneer Square going to and fro, most of them with earbuds and holding paper cups of coffee. Something Victoria said brought his attention back to the call.

"Could I speak to Margo while I'm waiting?" Victoria said, then covered the mouthpiece with her hand and informed Cross, "He's in the bathroom."

"How long has he been there?"

"For a few minutes," she said. "Margo is with him, too."

That was damn peculiar. Had they left the store somehow? Blackthorn had the block under visual surveillance from multiple angles. All the faces were being scanned by the facial recognition system so their targets wouldn't be lost in a crowd. Cross or the system would have seen Ludlow and French if they'd emerged onto the street anywhere on the same block.

But they hadn't showed.

Something on the screen caught his eye. Not a face, but a word. Cross tapped an icon on his touch screen and, in doing so, enlarged one of the camera feeds from Pioneer Square on the media wall. The camera was trained on the Victorian wrought-iron-and-glass cupola in the center of the cobblestone plaza. It was a bus stop. Behind the cupola/bus stop was a six-story, block-long sandstone building with a front entrance dominated by a masonry arch with PIONEER BUILDING etched into it. On either side of the arched entry were storefronts. Above one of the storefronts was a sign advertising THE UNDERGROUND TOUR.

Cross pointed to it. "Tell me about that."

Seth typed a query on his keyboard and looked at the result. "Pioneer Square is built above the old city. A small portion of the buried streets have been unearthed and restored for tours."

"What about the rest of the underground streets?" Cross asked.

"Most of them are filled in," Seth said, scanning the text on his screen, "but many are not."

"That's where Ludlow and French are," Cross said. "Show me all the access points to the underground."

A map of the underground was superimposed on a satellite image of Pioneer Square on the media wall. Blinking blue dots representing dozens of access points appeared on the image and were spread over several blocks.

"Those are all the ways in and out," Seth said. "Some are manholes on the streets and sidewalks, others are the basements of buildings."

"We've lost them," Victoria said.

Cross knew she was right. But it was only a temporary setback. Ludlow and French had to surface sometime in Seattle and it would be in front of a camera somewhere. It was inevitable and inescapable. It was a fact of modern life. Privacy was fast becoming obsolete. The key was to be ready to act when the moment came. He addressed the room.

"This is a priority-one fugitive search. Access every camera in the vicinity, public and private, live and recorded, and run everything through facial recognition until those two are found. Hack anything with a lens: security cameras, ATMs, taxis, smartphones, the Six Million Dollar Man's eyeball. Be creative and proactive. I want a deep dive into Margo French. Open her e-mail, her bank accounts, everything. No detail is too small. If she uses toothpaste, I want to know the brand and fluoride content." Cross turned to Victoria. "Get our asset on a plane to Seattle right now."

"What are the sanction parameters?"

"Put them both down," Cross said. "I don't care if it looks like an accident or natural causes anymore, as long as it doesn't look professional."

She nodded. "We'll leave a mess."

◎

Ian followed Margo up an iron ladder that led to a manhole cover. She pushed the cover up, slid it aside, and climbed out into the harsh sunlight. Margo waited on the edge of the hole to help Ian out. He emerged into a small park, with more hardscape than greenery, which had become a crowded homeless encampment filled with tents and makeshift shelters made of cardboard, plywood, and sheets of corrugated metal. None of the residents paid any attention to Ian and Margo.

She slid the manhole cover back into place, spotted a bus at the edge of the park, and swatted Ian on the shoulder. "That's our ride."

They ran to the bus and hopped inside just as the doors were about to close. Margo flashed a transit pass and Ian dumped all of the change in his pocket into the driver's hand. They found a seat in the back and hunkered down low, below the window frame. The bus lumbered forward.

They rode in silence, mostly because Ian fell asleep almost as soon as the bus started moving. After what felt like five seconds, Margo nudged him awake. He sat up, blinked hard, and saw they were no longer downtown. The bus stop was located in front of a cyclone fence that bordered what appeared to be sports fields and a nature preserve. On the opposite side of the road was the University Village shopping center. That landmark allowed Ian to get his bearings. They were northeast of downtown, between the University of Washington campus and the upscale Laurelhurst neighborhood on the western shore of Lake Washington.

They got off the bus and Ian stood for a moment, taking stock of himself and his situation. His mouth tasted like someone had used it for a urinal. His back ached from his unbalanced running. His broken right arm itched deep inside the cast. His good left arm was sore from overuse. And his head was pounding like his brain was desperate to escape. But he was alive and that was what counted.

He didn't see any cameras, though he knew there had to be some out there. But he didn't think the CIA was watching him now. Seattle was a big city and, at least for the moment, he believed his pursuers didn't know where to look.

But he wasn't fooling himself. Margo had bought them time to think, to take a breath, but they hadn't escaped.

Margo trudged up the street, east toward the residential neighborhood.

Ian hurried up alongside her. "Where are we going?"

"I'm a dog sitter. One of my clients lives up here, in a big house on the lake, and won't be back for three days. We can stay there."

"So you're a dog sitter, too."

He wasn't surprised to learn she had another job. There weren't enough authors coming through Seattle for her to make a living escorting them around.

"It's a lot like being an author escort," she said. "I feed the dogs, take them out, clean up their messes, and hope they won't hump my leg."

"I'm sensing a little hostility," Ian said.

"Gee, you think?" She shook her head, obviously dismayed by how clueless he was. "I totally get why someone wants to kill you."

"Why's that?"

"It's because you're a self-centered asshole."

"It has nothing to do with that."

She came to a sudden stop, turned, and got right into his face, almost nose to nose.

"You knew you were a target, but instead of going to the police, or hiding in a cave in Malibu, you came up here and let me take you around, knowing it would put me in the line of fire. That makes you a bona fide, self-centered asshole."

"I can see why you'd feel that way, but—"

"Asshole!" She shoved him hard and marched away.

Ian nearly fell, managed to regain his balance, and then rushed to catch up with her again. "You have it all wrong. I didn't know that anybody wanted me dead until yesterday."

She kept walking without looking at him. "What happened yesterday?"

"A plane crashed in Honolulu."

"Yeah, I know. Everybody does. What does that have to do with anything?"

He took a deep breath. He was about to take a big risk. Once she heard his story, there was a fifty-fifty chance that she'd walk out on him. If that happened, he was afraid there was a 100 percent chance that she'd be killed. But he had no choice. He had to tell her.

"It was my idea."

"Plane crashes happen all the time. It's not exactly an original idea."

Her flippant dismissal of his revelation was not the reaction he was expecting and it irritated him.

"Yes, so I've been told, but this crash is different. I know how it was done. It was one of the terrorism scenarios I came up with three years ago for the CIA."

"You're a writer," she said. "Why would the CIA want terrorism ideas from you?"

"I had the same question," he said.

CHAPTER FOURTEEN

Malibu, California. Three Years Ago.

Ian Ludlow's Spanish-style hacienda was nestled in the Santa Monica Mountains on a curving, secluded stretch of Mulholland Highway. It was a modest house, draped in bougainvillea and shaded by oaks.

The home was built and owned for decades by Dillon Harper, who starred in the TV series *Saddlesore* for its entire twenty-year run. That was one of the big reasons why Ian bought the house. He grew up watching Harper as the nameless bounty hunter who wandered the West, relentlessly hunting wanted men. By the time the show ended, Harper was as weather-beaten as a wooden barn and inseparable from the character he'd played. The actor, forever typecast as a Western hero, hardly worked after that. Harper's family eventually moved the senile, widowed old actor into a bungalow at the Motion Picture & Television Country Home in Woodland Hills and sold the house to Ian.

Living in a house once occupied by a television icon made Ian feel like he was part of Hollywood history himself, which was important to him, since he was sure he'd never earn a place in it based on his TV writing. He'd made money in Hollywood, but not a lasting mark.

Every so often, Dillon Harper would slip away from the retirement home, wander around the San Fernando Valley, and convince somebody to drive him to his hacienda on Mulholland. Ian would open his front door and Harper, wearing his cowboy hat, would stroll right in and head for the wet bar, believing that he still lived there. They'd always end up spending a few pleasant hours drinking Johnnie Walker Black Label and talking about *Saddlesore*. Then Ian would remind Harper that it was time to get to the studio and take him back to the retirement home.

So Ian's first thought when a black Suburban unexpectedly pulled up in front of his house that afternoon was that Harper was back again. It was perfect timing, too. Just moments before, Ian had been sitting in his office, struggling with the first paragraph of his new book and getting nowhere. In his misery, his gaze had drifted from his computer screen to his wall of framed TV screen credits, and then to his shelf of Clint Straker novels, for reassurance that he was actually capable of writing. Then he looked out his window and saw the Suburban arrive. He was delighted. It was the perfect excuse to spend the rest of the day drinking scotch with Harper and listening to his stories instead of trying to write one himself.

But Harper didn't step out of the Suburban. Instead, it was two guys in suits wearing those single earbuds that were common fashion accessories for cops, federal agents, and bodyguards on the job. Ian was intrigued. The men glanced around for threats, then opened the back door for their passenger, a man in his sixties wearing an Italian suit tailored to add some blunt edges to his roundish body. Ian decided the two guys were bodyguards and that the passenger was their boss. What kind of boss? His first thought was a mob boss, but he quickly dismissed it as the product of an overactive imagination. But it was a relief to know that he still had one.

One bodyguard remained standing outside the Suburban while the other one escorted their boss to Ian's door and knocked on it for him. This bodyguard was so thorough, Ian thought, he also protected his boss's tender knuckles.

Ian slipped his bare feet into the pair of sheepskin Uggs that were under his desk and, in his T-shirt and sweatpants, went to greet his mysterious guest. He opened the door to a big, friendly smile from the older man and a cold stare from the stony-faced bodyguard who stood behind him.

"Hello there," Ian said. "I don't suppose you're Jehovah's Witnesses."

"No, I'm not, Mr. Ludlow," the smiling man said. "Do you get a lot of them up here?"

"About as often as I get unexpected guests with bodyguards."

"I'd rather not travel with them but I'm afraid they're a requirement for a man in my position."

"If you were from the Publishers Clearing House sweepstakes, and you'd come to give me my million-dollar check, you'd have a camera crew," Ian said. "So I'm going to guess that aliens from another planet have landed and they've picked me as their intermediary to communicate with mankind."

"I'm a senior official at the Central Intelligence Agency. I flew here today from Washington, DC, to see you."

"That was my second guess," Ian said, a smile on his face. "So, why are you really here?"

"I wasn't joking," the man said. "I am with the CIA and we need your help."

At first, Ian thought the man was still joking but something about the steady way he held his gaze conveyed that he was serious. "What interest could the CIA possibly have in me?"

"That's what I'm here to explain. May I come in?"

"Yes, of course," Ian said, stepping aside. "I didn't get your name."

"You can call me Bob."

Bob came in but the bodyguard remained outside. Ian closed the door and led Bob into the living room, where two matching couches faced each other.

"Can I get you anything, Bob?" Ian resisted the urge to mime air quotes with his fingers when he said the mystery man's name.

"No, I'm fine, thank you."

Bob sat on one couch and Ian sat on the other, a wooden coffee table between them. Ian's couch faced the window so he could see past Bob to the CIA agent who was standing outside the SUV and staring at him. The agent was probably thinking of all the ways that he could kill Ian if necessary. Would the agent use his gun? His knife? Or his bare hands? Or perhaps the garrote sewn into the lining of his jacket? It was clear to Ian now that the best way to jump-start his imagination was to have a spy knock at his door. He'd have no trouble writing after this.

"I'll get right to the point, Mr. Ludlow. The CIA's job is to protect our nation, and further its objectives, by gathering intelligence and engaging in a wide range of covert actions. This responsibility includes anticipating potential threats and preventing enemy actions before they happen. That's where we need your experience and advice."

It was the craziest thing Ian had ever heard. He had no experience at all in espionage. Everything he knew about spying he got from watching James Bond movies and reading John le Carré novels. The only thing he was qualified to give advice on was writing, and even that was something he felt uncomfortable doing.

"I write thrillers, Bob. You live them. I don't see what I can tell you that would be remotely useful. I make stuff up. I don't actually know anything."

"The CIA is a vast organization of bureaucrats, analysts, and field operatives. We have the experience, the technical resources, and the special skills necessary to acquire vital information and act on it. What we lack is imagination."

Ian had lacked it, too, until Bob and his spies showed up. "Imagination is overrated, Bob. Trust me, you don't need a writer, certainly not this one."

"You're selling yourself short. You're a *New York Times* bestselling author and a writer for several top-rated TV shows. That makes you a member of an elite group with a singular talent. We want you and a few others to come and give us the benefit of your creativity," Bob said. "Successful writers like you have proven, time and time again, that you can create new, terrifying plots that connect emotionally with audiences worldwide. That's exactly what terrorists are striving to achieve."

"But what we come up with doesn't have to work in the real world," Ian said. "It just has to be entertaining."

"It doesn't matter. Your inventive plots will give us a fresh perspective, expose security loopholes we didn't know existed, and help us predict attacks that we couldn't possibly have imagined ourselves."

"You're saying that you need me, a man with a unique skill set, to save America."

"That's one way of putting it," Bob said.

It was ridiculous but Ian really liked the sound of it. He would be Liam Neeson in *Taken*, only shorter and carrying a pen instead of a gun.

"I'd be a covert operative whose top-secret mission is to make stuff up."

"That's a better way of putting it," Bob said.

The CIA wanted him to serve his country by hanging out with real-life spies and coming up with outrageous plots worthy of Bond villains. It was an amazing offer. The only downside was that this whole supercool experience would be a secret.

"I am so in," Ian said.

CHAPTER FIFTEEN

Seattle, Washington. July 18. 12:35 p.m. Pacific Standard Time.

"Two days later Bob flew me on a private jet to a cabin in Maine where I spent a weekend brainstorming catastrophe with three other writers," Ian said. "We had some fun, ate some great food, drank some terrific scotch, and I came home. I didn't hear from Bob or anybody else at the CIA again. I figured I did my patriotic duty and that was that."

He and Margo were walking through a neighborhood of large, expensive homes that overlooked Lake Washington. She'd been quiet while he'd told his story and now he waited for her reaction. She cleared her throat before she spoke.

"Let me get this straight. You believe the CIA carried out your terrorist plot and now they want to kill you to cover up their involvement."

Did he detect a hint of incredulity in her voice? "Yes, that's exactly what I think."

"That's absolutely ridiculous. No, it's beyond that. It's insane." He definitely detected some incredulity this time. "I'm sure there are much more believable reasons why someone is out to murder you. What do those other writers think about your theory?"

"They're dead," he said.

Margo stopped in front of a big Tudor-style brick house with half-timbered walls, pitched gables, diamond-paned windows, six chimneys, and a four-car garage.

"Dead how?" she asked.

"Drowning, heart attack, and drug overdose," Ian said. "All within a few weeks of one another and around the same time that I fell off a cliff and my house blew up."

Margo went up to the house as if she owned the place, used a key to open the front door, and then stepped inside the high-ceilinged foyer to type a code into the alarm panel on the wall. She faced him in the doorway.

"Make yourself at home," she said.

Ian went in and closed the door behind him. Two grand staircases curved up to the second floor in front of him and looked like they belonged in an opera house rather than a private home. The ostentatious display of wealth gave him some comfort. He was sure he'd be able to find some Vicodin or other opioids here.

He heard a rumble, and the scratching of nails on marble, and then two excited golden retrievers came bounding down the hall to greet Margo, jumping on her with delight. She was just as pleased to see them, petting them vigorously and whipping up a cloud of dog hair around her.

"Meet Kim and Kanye," she said. "They're sweeties."

The dogs didn't seem to care that Ian was there. Margo led the dogs and Ian down the hall and through a door into a huge kitchen that had every possible appliance, including a brick pizza oven. In the center of the kitchen was an enormous dining and cooking island under a rack of pots and pans that Ian guessed were mostly for decoration. The kitchen opened out into a surprisingly warm and inviting family room filled with overstuffed couches and chairs. The furniture was aligned to face the stone fireplace and the large flat-screen TV above it. French doors offered a fantastic view of Lake Washington and the perfectly manicured lawn that sloped gently down to a boathouse. There were worse places to hide out for the night.

"Did Bob show you his ID?" Margo asked, which told Ian that she was still seriously thinking about his story.

"Of course not. He's a spymaster. He isn't going to compromise his identity by flashing his ID or posting his espionage résumé on the web so he can be googled."

"Then how do you know he was really in the CIA?" Margo opened the french doors and the dogs bolted outside.

"Think about it," Ian said. "Who else besides the CIA has the resources to hack into cameras and cars?"

"You tell me," Margo said. "You're the guy with the wonderful imagination."

She walked outside and Ian did, too. He went down to the boathouse while the dogs peed and crapped on the lawn. Margo cleaned up after them with a pooper-scooper.

He walked to the end of the dock. The water lapped gently against the pilings. He watched a small seaplane land gracefully in the middle of the lake and glide like a haughty swan toward the Evergreen Point Floating Bridge. It was relaxing to stand there but his head still pounded and now his right shoulder ached from the weight of the cast. He unbuttoned his dress shirt halfway down, exposing his T-shirt underneath, and tucked his broken arm inside the opening like it was a big pocket. It eased the strain on his shoulder, though now the weight of the cast tugged his shirt collar tightly against the back of his neck. He couldn't win.

Margo dumped the dog poop into a garbage can, set the pooper-scooper down beside it, and joined Ian at the end of the dock. The dogs frolicked on the lawn, glad to be freed from the house.

"What was your plot to take control of the plane?" Margo said. "Did it involve Clint Straker seducing all of the stewardesses?"

"Passenger jets are big, flying Wi-Fi hot spots these days," Ian said. "Everybody on board can check their e-mails, tweet, and web surf. Even the plane itself is tweeting, constantly sending out data—"

Margo interrupted him. "I get it. Your idea was that the bad guys hack the plane. But in reality, there must be hardware barriers between the Wi-Fi stuff and flight control."

"What if the bad guys had people working on the aircraft assembly line? What if they put a tiny device deep inside the plane's wiring that bypasses those hardware barriers and allows the autopilot to be hacked by anyone with a Wi-Fi connection?"

"But you were just making shit up," she said. "There wasn't a device like that."

"There is now," he said.

CHAPTER SIXTEEN

The assassin amused herself on the short flight from Denver to Seattle, imagining all of the ways that she could murder the annoying woman in the next seat.

The trouble began before they took off. The woman boarded the plane late, yammering on her phone while holding a Starbucks coffee, lugging a huge shoulder bag, and dragging an overpacked rolling suitcase. She was a chubby fake blonde in her twenties wearing a pink tank top and black cobra-skin-patterned tights, a tacky outfit that accentuated her basketball boobs and bloated ass. The woman thrust her coffee cup into the assassin's hands without asking, then repeatedly bashed her in the head with her swinging shoulder bag as she shoved her suitcase into the overhead bin.

Once they were airborne, the woman cranked up the hip-hop on her earbuds loud enough for the assassin to hear and emptied her shoulder bag full of gossip magazines onto her lap and tray table. She flipped through the magazines and took possession of both armrests while eating from a bag of crunchy Cheetos that smelled like an endless fart.

It was as if the woman didn't see the assassin in the seat beside her. Of course, going unnoticed was something the assassin worked to achieve but she didn't appreciate suffering for it. Today the assassin was a slim, flat-chested woman wearing glasses and a gray pantsuit, her brown hair tied into an efficient bun. There was nothing memorable or remotely eye-catching about her.

The assassin traveled light, carrying a black jogging suit, running shoes, and some toiletries simply so she'd have something in her carry-on bag for the X-ray machine operator to see at airport security. She would buy or steal what she needed when she got to her destination and leave it all behind when she left. The assassin never carried weapons. She liked to improvise. It was what made her job fun. She understood why snipers enjoyed their work but it was too mechanical and distant for her. There wasn't any opportunity for spontaneity or creativity.

When the plane arrived in Seattle at 4:00 p.m., both the assassin and the woman, her clothes now covered with a fine layer of yellow Cheetos dust, took the courtesy bus to the car rental terminal. Once there, the assassin used a stolen credit card at E-Z Rent a Car to book a compact Kia and was heading for the parking structure with her suitcase when she saw the annoying woman go into the restroom. It was too inviting an opportunity for the assassin to pass up. The assassin followed her inside.

The four stalls were open and unoccupied. The woman stood at the sink, washing the yellow Cheetos dust off her greasy hands. The assassin left her suitcase beside the door, came up behind the woman, and spoke in a voice barely above a whisper.

"Don't worry about your hands. The mortician will clean them."

"Huh?" the woman said.

The assassin grabbed the woman's head and gave it a sharp twist, breaking her neck with an audible snap. She caught the woman by her armpits, dragged her into the nearest stall, and sat her on the toilet. Then she went back to the sink and gave the woman's suitcase a kick, sending it rolling into the stall. She took a paper towel, reached up to the top of the stall door, and pulled it closed. The whole encounter lasted sixty-eight seconds.

It wasn't one of the ways the assassin had imagined killing the woman but it was still satisfying. The assassin washed her hands, grabbed her suitcase, and walked out to her car.

Ian was right: There was Vicodin in the house. He found a prescription bottle upstairs in the master bedroom medicine cabinet. The tablets had expired six months earlier so he dry-swallowed two to make up for any lack of potency, washed his mouth out with Listerine, and went back down the ridiculous staircase to the kitchen, where Margo was making herself a smoked salmon sandwich. He made one, too, sat on the couch to eat it, and fell asleep after his second bite.

It was dark outside when he awoke. One of the dogs was lying across his lap. His head wasn't pounding anymore, his backache was gone, and even his arm wasn't itching in the cast. The Vicodin had worked its magic.

Margo sat in an easy chair, smoking a joint and watching CNN on the TV. Did she bring the pot, he asked himself, or had she found some in the house? One of the dogs was at her feet, chewing on a rubber lobster. A crustacean didn't strike Ian as a logical doggie chew toy but what did he know? Perhaps it was lobster flavored.

Ian petted the dog on his lap. "Which one is this?"

"Kim."

"I think she likes me."

"She likes sleeping on the couch," she said.

Okay, he thought, so Margo is still pissed at me. Not that he could blame her.

On the TV, Wolf Blitzer was talking with CNN's aviation expert, Shawn Danielson, in the studio. The ticker-tape-style headlines running along the bottom of the screen reported that the downed flight's data and voice recorders had been recovered from the wreckage.

> **BLITZER:** The aircraft that went down in Honolulu is a Gordon-Ganza 877, the new, lighter, more fuel-efficient model of the company's 876, the workhorse of many major airlines. How safe is this new plane?

> **DANIELSON:** That's a good question. This is the second tragedy related to the new aircraft, the first being the disappearance of Indonesian Air Flight 230 on its way to Hong Kong. But I don't think the issue is the plane.

> **BLITZER:** Data transmitted automatically by the aircraft indicated that the autopilot was activated shortly after takeoff. Doesn't that contradict the copilot, who said in his final transmission that the plane was out of control?

> **DANIELSON:** Not necessarily. Someone programmed the autopilot, activated it, and kept it on. The simple explanation is that one of the pilots is responsible. The alternative is sabotage.

> **BLITZER:** Which possibility do you find more frightening?

> **DANIELSON:** Sabotage. Because if they did it once . . . they could do it again.

"What have you been doing while I've been asleep?" Ian asked.

"Thinking." Margo used the remote to mute the TV. "This is really fucked."

"Yeah," he said.

"Over three hundred people are dead, almost a thousand are injured. Why would our own government do that?"

"I don't know," Ian said.

"It didn't come up in your brainstorming sessions?"

"We were thinking up attacks that terrorists might carry out against us," Ian said. "Not our own government."

"We need to go to the police."

"We can't."

"Why not?"

"We're up against the CIA," Ian said. "But why stop there? The Pentagon and the White House could be involved, too. If we walk into a police station, I guarantee you that we'll be found dead the next morning, even if we were in protective custody."

"You can't guarantee that because you don't know shit about what the CIA can or can't do. You're a writer. You make stuff up."

"That's right. But here's what I do know. They were able to crash an airplane into Waikiki by remote control. They knew exactly where we were. They were watching us every second. They were able to locate a car with autopilot, hack it, and try to run me over with it. That tells me that they can reach us and kill us anywhere."

"That means we aren't safe no matter where we go," she said. "So unless you come up with a better alternative by morning, I'll take my chances with the police. At least I'll be surrounded by men with guns."

And they could be pointed at you, Ian thought. But he didn't say that. She was right. He needed a survival plan and he didn't have one yet.

"I'm sorry I got you involved in this," he said.

Margo got up without acknowledging the apology. "The dogs have been fed. They'll want to go out again. You'll have to handle that. I'm going to bed."

"Sweet dreams," Ian said.

"Yeah, like that's going to happen." She trudged out of the room.

CHAPTER SEVENTEEN

Seattle's fleet of metro buses were equipped with security cameras that recorded eight hours of video onto a hard drive. The video was automatically uploaded to the server when the buses returned to the transit yard for gas or service. That's why it wasn't until about 8:00 p.m. Pacific Standard Time that the video showing Ian and Margo riding the bus from downtown to Laurelhurst landed on the server. It was another forty-five minutes before the video was swept up by Blackthorn's search bot and sifted by their facial recognition system. The instant the system identified Ian and Margo, a screen grab appeared on the media wall in the situation room, accompanied by a shrill alert beep that got everyone's attention.

Things moved swiftly after that. The Blackthorn operatives remotely accessed the footage recorded that day by cameras at University Village, Burgermaster, the Center for Urban Horticulture, and other businesses near the bus stop on northeast Forty-Fifth Street. Using that video, they were able to visually track Ian and Margo as they walked to northeast Forty-First Street but lost sight of them once the pair was in the residential neighborhood.

But that was only a temporary setback. Seth searched the recent incoming calls to Margo's cell phone and uncovered one from Sam

Barber, the owner of a maritime shipping company, who lived in Laurelhurst, owned two dogs, and was presently in Beijing with his wife. He figured Margo had to be their dog sitter.

It was an easy assumption to confirm. The Barbers had an alarm system that was monitored by a subsidiary of Blackthorn. A review of the Barbers' activity logs showed that someone opened the front door, and entered the alarm deactivation code, ten minutes after Blackthorn lost visual surveillance of Ian and Margo.

Shortly after 4:00 a.m. Eastern Standard Time, Victoria called Wilton Cross, who was sleeping in his office apartment, to let him know that the targets had been located.

The assassin was staying at a Red Roof Inn, two blocks from the rental car terminal and across the street from a cemetery, in a ground-floor room with a view of a gas station.

When she'd arrived that afternoon, she removed her glasses, blue-colored contact lenses, and brown wig, stripped off her dull gray pantsuit, and unwound the ace bandages that she'd wrapped around her chest to flatten her breasts. The assassin was now a short-haired, busty blonde with green eyes. She yanked the filthy comforter and blanket off the double bed and rested naked on the clean white sheets to wait for instructions.

They didn't come until late that night. Her throwaway phone vibrated on the nightstand. She picked it up and checked the message screen. It was a text with DMV photos of Ian Ludlow and Margo French and a hyperlinked Seattle address. She tapped the address and a satellite map came up with a targeting dot on the location. It was a lakefront home on East Laurelhurst Drive.

She picked up her suitcase, unpacked the black jogging suit, and got dressed to kill.

Ian spent the night on the couch, drinking Johnnie Walker from the bottle, eating cashews from a huge Costco jar, and watching reruns of old TV shows, seeking comfort and safety in the company of his good friends Thomas Magnum, Joe Mannix, and Walker, Texas Ranger. Those were guys who knew how to handle problems. So was Clint Straker, and so were *Hollywood & the Vine* and every other character that Ian wrote about. So why was he having such a hard time figuring out what to do next? If he could come up with crime stories for a man who was half-plant, surely he could think of something he could do to outwit his opponents. Thinking about *Hollywood & the Vine* actually gave him an idea, one that might help them survive, but probably wouldn't convince Margo not to go to the police. Still, at least now he knew what to do in the morning but that was still a few hours away.

That's when one of the dogs nudged his good arm with her wet nose and whined at him while the other dog scratched at the french door. How long had they been asking to go out? He set the half-empty bottle of Johnnie Walker and the jar of nuts on the coffee table, got up on shaky legs, and opened the french doors for the dogs.

At the same instant that Ian opened that door, another door opened at the back of the kitchen. The assassin slipped into the house from the side yard, unnoticed by man or beast. She casually selected a knife from a wooden knife block on the counter and crept up behind Ian, who stood at the open french door, his back to her. This would be easier than killing a fly.

Ian started to close the french door when he saw a reflection in one of the windowpanes and screamed. He saw a woman behind him, raising a knife to his throat. He whirled around to face her, instinctively bringing up his right arm, the one in a cast, to protect himself. Her blade raked the cast as he clumsily backed away from her, still screaming.

The assassin advanced, swinging and thrusting the knife. He blocked her repeatedly with his cast, the blade stabbing through the plaster, chipping away at it. She was smiling the whole time and he realized, to his horror, that the only reason he was still alive was because she was amused by his ridiculous attempts at self-defense. But she was getting tired of it.

She kicked his legs out from under him. He fell onto the coffee table and she came in for the kill. He grabbed the whiskey bottle by the neck with his good hand and swung it at her head. She raised her arm to block the blow. The bottle smashed against her arm, cutting her and splashing them both with whiskey. Her eyes became ice cold and he knew he was going to die.

Ian's screams brought Margo running into the kitchen while he was still fighting off the assassin. She grabbed two frying pans, one in each hand, from the overhead rack and charged into the family room. The assassin turned away from Ian just as Margo swung a frying pan at her head. The assassin dodged the pan and thrust her knife at Margo, who blocked it with the other frying pan. Now the assassin directed her fury at Margo, leaving Ian behind.

Margo deflected the assassin's knife attacks with the frying pans. But the assassin kept coming, with increasing speed and ferocity, forcing Margo back against the cooking island. In a second, Ian was certain that Margo would be pinned and killed.

Ian got to his feet, grabbed a fireplace poker, and charged the assassin. She sensed him coming and seemed more irritated than threatened. She turned to face him just as the two golden retrievers came bounding back into the house, right across Ian's path.

Ian tripped over the dogs and flew forward, straight into the assassin, driving the poker into her stomach with the force of his full body weight. Her body made a moist, sucking sound as she was gored and he felt the sickening, gelatinous sensation of her flesh being penetrated.

He let go of the poker and scrambled away. The assassin stared at him with profound disbelief, blood spilling out of her belly, and toppled to the floor.

CHAPTER EIGHTEEN

An Excerpt from *Death Benefits* by Ian Ludlow

The barbecue joint was on a desolate highway in a forgotten corner of Texas. The only sign was a piece of warped, cracked plywood with the three letters *BBQ* painted in faded red. There were no posted hours. The shack began serving when the meat was ready and closed when the meat was gone.

The cinder block and corrugated metal shack was filled with smoke from the pits out back, where racks of ribs and brisket were barbecued to perfection. The pit master was an ancient black man, his face weathered from decades spent leaning into the heat and smoke, his stained apron the painted history of Texas barbecue. The pit master lived in a double-wide behind the shack. The meat was his life.

Straker was the only customer. He sat at one of the two long wooden picnic tables, each covered with throwaway red-checkerboard tablecloths. He took a fork and knife from the mason jar full of cutlery in the center of the table and set them on the white paper napkin beside his bottle of beer.

The waitress came out with a plate of pork ribs, a bowl of beans, and a piece of homemade bread that was torn from the loaf with her bare hands. She was a middle-aged white woman with big cheeks—front and rear—and a clean apron.

"I hope the ribs taste as good as they smell," Straker said.

"Even better, honey." She gestured to the three squeeze bottles on the table, each a different shade of red. "Those are the sauces. Original, spicy, and Melt Your Fucking Face Off."

Straker reached for the Melt Your Fucking Face Off, slathered a rib with it, and took a bite. The waitress watched for the agonized reaction, and got none. She was bewildered.

"It's mighty tasty," Straker said. "But I have toothpaste with more kick."

"I must have put the wrong sauce in the bottle." She squeezed a drop of the Melt Your Fucking Face Off onto her fingertip, licked it, and instantly winced with pain. "What do you brush your teeth with? Lye?"

Before he could answer, three big shitkickers carrying baseball bats stepped into the joint. They wore sleeveless shirts and tank tops that showed off their prison tats and jailhouse muscles. One stood at the door while the other two approached Straker. The waitress stepped away from the table but Straker concentrated on eating his first rib.

"We come to teach you a lesson, boy," Shitkicker #1 said, standing to Straker's right.

"It's *we've* come," Straker said. "Now I've just taught you a lesson."

"Get up, asshole," Shitkicker #2 said, standing to Straker's left.

"I'm eating lunch." Straker finished his first rib and set down the clean bone. "Wait outside and you can frighten me when I'm done."

"We ain't gonna frighten you, boy," Shitkicker #3 said from his spot at the door. "We're gonna beat the shit out of you."

"Then I suggest you call for some more men while you're waiting," Straker said, reaching for the squeeze bottle of Melt Your Fucking Face Off.

"There's three of us and one of you," Shitkicker #1 said.

"You're outnumbered." Straker squirted the sauce into Shitkicker #1's face. It didn't melt the man's face off but he screamed in pain and reached for his eyes.

Straker grabbed the top of Shitkicker #1's bat with both hands and jammed the handle deep into the man's gut. Shitkicker #1 doubled over and dropped to the floor, banging his head on the edge of the table as he went down. Straker set the bat on the bench.

Shitkicker #2 charged, bat above his head. Straker whirled around and threw his fork at him like it was a dagger. The fork plunged deep into Shitkicker #2's throat. The man instinctively grabbed for the fork and dropped his bat. Straker caught the bat, rammed Shitkicker #2 in the balls with it, and then set it on the bench, too. Shitkicker #2 hit the floor, curled up in agony beside his friend.

Straker hadn't moved from his seat or disturbed his plate. He looked at the shitkicker who stood at the door and said, "Can I finish my lunch now?"

"Yeah, sure," the man stammered and walked out the door.

Straker put some sauce on his ribs, had a sip of his beer, and got back to eating, paying no attention to the two men on the floor as they struggled to their feet and staggered out of the place. They left their bats behind.

The waitress came over and set a thick slice of pecan pie on the table. "We're going to have to rename our hot sauce."

"Why's that?" Straker asked.

"Billy Bob may be blind for life but he's still got his face," she said. "You have any suggestions?"

Straker wiped his lips with his napkin. "The Ass Kicker."

CHAPTER NINETEEN

The assassin's death was agonizing and ugly. Blood gushed out of her belly and bubbled up out of her mouth. She gurgled and her body twitched. Her bladder and bowels emptied with a noisy splurt and a revolting stench. The next instant, she was suddenly as still and lifeless as a rock.

This was a real death, unlike anything Ian had ever seen, because he'd seen only fictional death before. But now that she was dead, he slowly became aware of his own trembling, of the dogs cowering behind the couch, and of Margo beside him, staring numbly at the body and holding a pan in each hand, prepared for more battle. Ian gently touched Margo's hand, snapping her out of her stare.

"I don't think you need those anymore," he said.

Margo became aware of herself and hung the scratched and dented pans back on the rack.

"That's the second time you saved my life," he said.

Margo shook her head. "We saved each other."

An actual, professional assassin had tried to kill them both and he'd killed her instead. It was unbelievable. But there she was, right in front of him. He could see her and smell her. Somehow seeing an actual killer, especially a dead one, lying on the floor in front of him made the danger more visceral. It was one thing to have a car trying to run him over, but quite another to see the threat against him in the flesh. He'd looked a killer in the eye this time, not a camera lens. The threat against him was amorphous before. Now it was human.

But who was this killer? Where did she come from? And how did she find them?

One of the dogs, feeling emboldened, inched forward to sniff at the blood. Margo grabbed the dog by the collar and pulled him back. "No, no, no. Stay away from the dead psychopath."

"You should get the dogs out of here," Ian said. "And keep them out."

"Yeah, that's a good idea."

Margo hustled the dogs out of the kitchen into the dining room and closed the doors, then came back in and closed the french doors leading outside.

While she did that, Ian went to the sink, put a rubber dish glove on his left hand, and crouched beside the assassin's body, careful not to get blood, or anything else, on his shoes. He reached out with his left hand and began easing a fanny pack out from under her body, wincing as he did it and breathing through his mouth to avoid the stink.

Margo squatted beside him, grimacing at the gore. "What are you doing?"

"I saw this fanny pack on her when she went after you. I want to see what she's got inside. Maybe we can learn something about who she was and how she found us."

He unzipped the bloody pack, holding it at arm's length, and carefully removed a rental car key fob, a lock pick, and a disposable cell phone. He stood up, flipped the phone open, and showed Margo what was on the message screen. His hand was shaking so she had to grab his wrist to steady the phone while she looked at the display. She saw pictures of the two of them and the address of the house.

"How did they find us?" she asked.

"I don't know," he said. "But I'm going to try to buy us some time."

He took off his glove and typed a two-word text back to whoever had sent the photos and address:

It's done.

Blackthorn Global Security Headquarters, Bethesda, Maryland. July 19. 5:17 a.m. Eastern Standard Time.

Victoria was half-asleep on the vinyl couch in the employee break room, her phone clutched in her hand, her head on the hard armrest. Her phone vibrated, waking her up. She opened her eyes and squinted at her text screen.

It's done.

She smiled. About fucking time.

Seattle, Washington. July 19. 2:18 a.m. Pacific Standard Time.

Ian powered off the phone the instant he got the "delivered" tag on the text message. He went to the sink and dropped the phone into the disposal.

Margo followed him. "What was the point of that?"

"I've either convinced them we're dead or did something so outside of their regular protocol that they'll know we're still alive." Ian ran the faucet and turned on the disposal. It chewed the phone with a labored grinding and then jammed up with a mechanical whine. He turned off the disposal and shut off the water. "Either way, I hope it bought us a few hours."

"To do what?"

"Run," he said.

He started for the door that led to the entry hall.

"Wait." Margo gestured to the assassin. "Aren't we going to clean this up?"

"Hell no. We need to get as far away from here as we can and we don't have time to waste." He opened the door, careful not to let the dogs in. "Are you coming?"

She nodded and walked out with him. "I'm going to get a terrible review on Yelp."

It was a funny thing to say and he found it reassuring because it told him several important things:

1. She was a fighter.
2. She had her shit together.
3. She was going to stay with him and not go running to the police.
4. She understood they were both fucked.

"They're dead." Victoria called Cross, waking him up for a second time that night to tell him the news.

"Finally," Cross said.

He hung up the phone, settled back into the sumptuous bed in his office apartment, and thought about what he'd done and what was yet to come.

From an operational standpoint, he was glad that Ludlow and French were dead. But he took no pleasure in killing them or the hundreds of people in Honolulu. They were all innocent civilians. But it had to be done for the greater good.

He considered himself a patriot and for years it had sickened and disturbed him to see the CIA's resources and abilities decay due to bureaucratic incompetence, political cowardice, and public apathy while the terrorist threat to America intensified. On top of that, the agency was crippled by ridiculous legal restrictions imposed on it by people more concerned with privacy and civil liberties than with the survival of the country.

The answer was obvious to Cross: Give the CIA's job to Blackthorn. They had the technology, the people, and the freedom to do it right. But it wouldn't happen through politics as usual. The biggest hurdles wouldn't be getting the public to agree to the outsourcing of the CIA's key responsibilities to Blackthorn or dramatically limiting the government's oversight into their activities. It would be repealing all of the laws and international treaties that stood in the way of America doing its necessary spying, stealing, and killing effectively.

To make it happen, Cross used history as his guide. It had taken 9/11 to get the Patriot Act passed, and with it the sweeping relaxation of civil liberties that gave domestic law enforcement agencies the broad, and deeply intrusive, surveillance powers they'd sought for decades. It also made the government secretly eager to go far beyond that, at least until Edward Snowden ruined things.

Cross knew it would take another attack, one that terrified the public and outraged politicians, to expose the CIA's impotence and give the president the moral imperative to give Blackthorn the nation's covert operations, free of any legal or bureaucratic restraints.

Ludlow came up with the idea of the plane crash, and how to do it, but it was Cross who refined the plan and targeted Hawaii so it would echo back in the nation's consciousness to 9/11 and Pearl Harbor.

Cross had crashed that plane for the good of the country and, yes, for the money it would bring to Blackthorn. He didn't think the windfall profits clashed with his patriotic motivations. Blackthorn would spend the money better, and more productively, for the security of the nation than the CIA would.

And why shouldn't he, and the people who worked for Blackthorn, be generously compensated for the hazardous duty they undertook, personal sacrifices they made, and emotional burdens they endured on behalf of their country?

No one deserved that compensation more than he, the man ultimately responsible for the deaths of hundreds of innocent men, women, and children. He'd need all the luxuries and indulgences money could buy to help him live with that. Not that he had any regrets about doing it. The dead were patriots who'd sacrificed their lives for the future safety and prosperity of their families and their country. In his business, he firmly believed the ends justified the means.

But when he pulled up his sheets, laid his face on his soft pillow, and tried to imagine those nubile nymphs sewing his Egyptian sheets, the only faces that came to his mind were those of the screaming passengers of TransAmerican 976.

It only proved to him how much he deserved all of that money.

CHAPTER TWENTY

Seattle, Washington. July 19. 2:20 a.m. Pacific Standard Time.

"Your cast is falling apart," Margo said as they walked out of the kitchen. "Come with me."

Ian looked at his right arm. The cast was crumbling, riddled with gashes from the knife, and barely hanging together. Some of the gauze underneath the plaster was bloodstained where the assassin's knife had pierced his skin. He didn't think any of the cuts were very deep, but even if they were, the cast would probably be an adequate bandage. He based that on the medical knowledge he'd gained from watching Dr. Dick Van Dyke on *Diagnosis: Murder.*

She led him to the laundry room, which was the size of a one-bedroom apartment and fitted with the same custom cabinetry as the kitchen. In addition to a high-end washer and dryer, there was also a steam press, an ironing station, a sewing station, and other equipment that Ian assumed was for dry cleaning. There was a center island for folding laundry, with a wide roll of tissue paper on a dispenser at one end.

Margo sat him down at a stool at the island, opened one of the nearby cabinets, and pulled out a roll of duct tape and a pair of scissors.

"How many people live in this house?" Ian asked.

She sat down next to him and began wrapping silver duct tape tightly around his cast. "Just the two of them. Eight people, tops, when their kids, their spouses, and the grandchildren stay over."

Ian shook his head. "They could start a business out of this room, doing laundry for the entire neighborhood."

"It's ridiculous," she said. "Some people don't know what to do with all of their money."

"Now that you mention it, we need money."

"*I* need money," she said. "You're loaded."

"I'm rich but I don't carry around wads of cash. I use plastic for everything. I've only got about two hundred dollars on me. What have you got?"

"Ten bucks."

"We need more."

"Don't look at me," she said. "That ten bucks is nearly all of my liquid assets."

"We aren't going to get very far without money. But we can't use our credit cards or go to an ATM or they'll know exactly where we are. We also can't go to family or friends. The CIA will be watching them all."

"So what are we going to do?" she said. "Steal stuff from here and hock it?"

Ian shook his head. "Pawn shops have surveillance cameras and the CIA is probably watching the pawn shops, too."

"They can't watch everything."

"They can come pretty close," Ian said. "And they probably have experts who are trying to anticipate our next move, based on their experience and detailed psychological assessments of us that they're putting together using everything they're learning about us from our school records, medical records, social media, tax returns, you name it."

"You're making that up."

"Yes, I am but does it sound credible to you?"

"Yes," she said.

"Then let's assume I'm right," Ian said. "Everybody has some loose cash in their house so there must be some here. We have to find it."

"I'll start looking for the money." She cut off the tape with scissors and patted the last strip down on his now silver cast. "You need to take a shower and change your clothes."

"We don't have time for that," he said.

"You can't go out in public reeking of whiskey and BO in soiled clothes you've been wearing for two days."

"I don't smell that bad," he said.

"You also look like a mass murderer," she said. "Anybody who sees you will scream and call the police."

"Because my hair is a little messy and I haven't shaved? It's the grunge look. It started right here in Seattle, where mass murderer Ted Bundy killed a bunch of women and he looked like a lawyer."

"That's true," she said. "But your clothes are spattered with blood and that never creates a positive first impression."

Ian looked down at himself, saw the red spots, and remembered the moist sound the poker made going into the assassin's stomach. He shivered.

"Okay, you have a point."

"Take off your shirt," she said.

He did as he was told, working his cast back through the right sleeve. It wasn't easy getting shirts on and off with his arm bent at a ninety-degree angle and encased in plaster . . . and now duct tape, too.

Margo went to another cabinet and pulled out two Hefty trash bags. She stuffed his stained shirt into one of the bags and pulled the

Lee Goldberg

other one over his cast, then used the duct tape to tape it closed at his shoulder.

"Now you can shower," she said. "Take the bag off when you're done."

"You've had experience with this."

"I broke both of my arms when I was a kid," she said. "I sucked at soccer."

"Soccer is played with your feet."

"Not the way I played," she said.

Ian went up to the master bathroom, which was about a thousand square feet of marble and had a steam shower for two and a Jacuzzi for six that was fed by a waterfall. He undressed, stuffed his underwear, pants, and socks in the Hefty bag, and took a shower at the hottest temperature he could stand.

As hot as it was, he started shivering again. He'd killed a person tonight. It wasn't guilt over taking a life that shook him up and it wasn't because he was afraid of consequences he might face. It was the realization that he was something he wasn't before. Before he was a screenwriter and an author. Now he was also a killer. It wasn't something he'd trained for or expected. It was something that happened to him. Something that had changed him. He was shaking like a butterfly emerging from its cocoon. How it had changed him was something he didn't know yet and didn't have the time to worry about. Right now he had to keep looking ahead, not backward or inward.

Steadied by his new resolve, Ian got out of the shower, removed the wet bag from his arm, gargled with Listerine, and rummaged through the man of the house's five-hundred-square-foot closet for some fresh clothes. He quickly learned that Brooks Brothers got most of the guy's clothing business. The guy also owned several blazers with yachting, fraternity, and golf club crests on the breast pocket, which made him a douchebag. He probably owned a few cravats, too. The guy was a little taller and heavier than Ian. But if Ian tucked in the shirts and rolled up the sleeves, they fit fine, especially over his cast. He had to keep his own shoes, though, because the guy had tiny feet.

Ian got dressed, stuffed some extra clothes, toiletries, and the Vicodin into an overnight bag, and lugged it and his trash bag downstairs, resisting the childish urge to slide down the huge curved railing of the grand staircase. The last thing he needed now was to break his other arm, too.

He found Margo emptying a huge bag of dry dog food into a pile in the center of the living room beside a bucket of water. The two dogs watched her but seemed bewildered, their heads cocked and their ears up. It was a crazy night for all of them.

"Don't eat this all at once," she told the dogs and then walked over to Ian. "Do you know how to crack a safe?"

"Nope," he said.

"Clint Straker would."

"Sorry to disappoint you," he said.

"I found a big safe that's probably full of money, hidden behind a painting. But since you can't open it, we'll have to settle for this." She led him to a table in the entry hall, where she'd placed a Costco cashew jar full of pocket change. "I found it in the master bedroom closet, where they probably empty their pockets each night. There's probably a couple of hundred dollars in there. And we've got this."

She picked up a leather travel wallet that was beside the jar and handed it to him. "I found it in Mr. Barber's desk drawer."

The wallet was filled with euros, Canadian dollars, British pounds, and about five hundred American dollars in twenty-dollar bills.

"Good job," Ian said. "That should hold us for a while. Now we need transportation."

Ian headed down the hall to the garage. Margo grabbed the jar of coins and followed him.

The garage was immaculate, with white walls and a polished concrete floor. There were four cars for them to choose from, all gleaming like they were in a showroom: a 2017 two-door Ferrari twin turbo 488GTB, a 2015 four-door Porsche Panamera, a 2016 Range Rover SUV, and a mint-condition 1968 Mustang 390 GT fastback in highland green like the one Steve McQueen drove in *Bullitt*. The keys to the cars were on a pegboard on the wall.

Margo made a beeline for the Ferrari, reconsidered, and moved to the sensible Range Rover.

Ian shook his head. "Wrong choice."

"It's a big, roomy car and not something flashy that will attract the police. We can even sleep in it if we have to."

"I appreciate the practicality of the Range Rover but we don't want any cars with electronics that can be hacked or tracked. That rules out all the cars but one."

He snatched a key chain with a running-pony logo on it from the pegboard and went to the Mustang. The car didn't have a single electronic component. And if it was good enough for Steve McQueen, it would be good enough for him.

He popped the trunk and they stuffed their things inside. Then he went to the driver's side of the car. He was relieved to see it was an automatic transmission, not a stick, which would have been impossible for him to drive with a broken arm.

It made much more sense for Margo to do the driving, especially since, technically, she was still his author escort. But he was taking charge of this operation and she was glad to let him. It allowed him to sustain the illusion that he had a master plan, which he didn't. He was acting on panic and some of the things that he'd learned writing cop shows and Clint Straker novels. All he knew for sure was where they were headed but he had no idea what would happen after that.

He asked Margo for directions to the seediest part of town. She told him how to get there and he drove up and down dark alleys until he found an abandoned pickup truck sitting on blocks. He parked behind it and, at his direction, Margo swapped their license plates for the ones on the truck. Then Margo peeled off the current registration stickers from the Mustang's original plates and affixed them to the former truck plates with folded pieces of duct tape from Ian's cast. This was all done to protect their asses. Ian didn't want to get pulled over by the highway patrol for driving a stolen car or having expired plates. They tossed the Hefty bag full of Ian's bloody clothes into a trash bin, and as dawn began to break on the Jet City, Ian drove onto the I-5 South.

He was a man on the run, though careful not to exceed the fifty-five-miles-per-hour speed limit.

CHAPTER TWENTY-ONE

It had been a rough forty or so hours since the seven senators last sat in this chamber and first heard about the catastrophic crash of TransAmerican 976. Now they were back again, weary and anxious, to listen to a classified briefing on the situation from acting CIA director Michael Healy, who sat alone at the witness table.

Healy was a career CIA employee, recruited while he was a student at Harvard, studying foreign relations, who rose over the course of nearly two decades from analyst to deputy director. He was a Mormon and so clean-cut in appearance and lifestyle that he could have risen to the top at Disneyland, though the two jobs did have some things in common: Both were Mickey Mouse operations that took place in a world of their own.

Five weeks ago, the president had appointed Healy as the agency's acting director after his boss was forced to resign in scandal when the *Washington Post* had revealed that the decorated former general, married father of four, and grandfather of two had been having a long-term affair with a field agent's young wife. The airplane crash in Hawaii was the first major crisis Healy had to face as the man in charge, and at that moment, he would have preferred to be seating people in a bobsled for the Matterhorn ride.

Senator Ramsey Holbrook, the chairman of the committee, got right to the point. "Is this an accident or another 9/11?"

"It's still too early to tell, Mr. Chairman," Healy said. "We didn't hear any uptick in chatter about a pending terrorist attack prior to the crash nor are we hearing anything now that points to a particular party being responsible."

"What actions are you taking?"

"We're doing 'molecular-level' deep-background checks on all of the passengers and crew for ties to overseas terrorist groups or foreign actors. We're also exerting intense pressure on our intelligence sources worldwide."

Senator Sam Tolan sighed, releasing more indignation than air. "So you were taken completely off guard and you're still in the dark, playing catch-up."

"These things happen," Healy said.

"Not if our intelligence agencies are doing their jobs," Tolan snapped back.

Holbrook spoke up quickly in an effort to keep Tolan, who'd made his name as a showboating prosecutor in Houston, from hijacking the briefing. "What are the NTSB, Homeland Security, and the FBI telling you about what they've learned?"

Healy grimaced. "They've shut us out. They like to remind us that we're legally barred from conducting domestic intelligence activities."

"You're the director of the goddamned C-I-fucking-A," Tolan said. "You should know what they know before they know it."

Senator Kelly Stowe, the liberal Californian, looked down the rostrum at Tolan. "Are you suggesting that the CIA spy on government agencies?"

"This is an attack on America, Senator," Tolan said. "It should be all hands on deck, interagency rivalries and petty legalities be damned."

"I couldn't agree more," Healy said.

"Then why the hell don't you do something about it?" Tolan said.

An aide came into the chamber, approached Senator Holbrook, and whispered something in his ear. Holbrook nodded and addressed the witness.

"Director Healy. I've been informed that Wilton Cross is here. He says he has urgent information for the committee and you. Do you mind if he joins us?"

Yes, he most certainly did mind. Healy knew who Cross was, of course. They'd worked together when Cross was at the agency. They'd had frequent, heated disagreements over procedure. Healy thought procedure should be followed, while Cross had a more flexible interpretation, as well as more pliable ethics. Healy was glad when Cross left the agency for the private sector.

So Healy dreaded what was about to come. He knew that the only reason Cross would intrude on this meeting was if he intended to stab Healy in the back, slit his throat, and shit on his corpse as he bled out.

What Healy didn't know was that his imminent humiliation had actually been set in motion months before when Blackthorn anonymously revealed his predecessor's affair to a reporter at the *Washington Post*. Cross didn't want the former director, a far more experienced intelligence professional, at the helm of the CIA when TransAmerican 976 went down.

"It's your hearing, Mr. Chairman," Healy said, graciously bowing to the inevitable. "Mr. Cross still has top secret security clearance."

The senator whispered some words to his aide, who nodded and stepped out. A moment later, Cross entered from the back of the room with Seth Barclay, who was holding a stack of files. Healy was familiar with Seth, too, since Cross had poached him from the CIA shortly after he left to run covert ops at Blackthorn. Cross joined Healy at the witness table while Seth handed out the files to the senators.

Healy shook Cross' hand and smiled with false warmth. "Good morning, Will."

"Sorry for barging in on you, Mike. But I thought you should hear this, too."

"Dramatic entrances aren't usually your style."

"These are unusual times," Cross said and handed Healy a file. Both men sat down. Cross waited until Seth left the room before speaking. "I'll get right to it, gentlemen. We know who crashed the plane and how it was done."

There were gasps of surprise from the senators and a look of barely restrained fury from Healy, who knew that his career at the CIA was over. He not only stood zero chance of being nominated as the actual director but now it would be impossible for him to keep his position as deputy director, too. Even so, he knew the shit had only begun to land on his corpse. He braced himself for a herd of elephants to empty their bowels on him.

"I will start at the beginning," Cross said. "Two Syrian Americans, Ayoub Darwish and Habib Ebrahimi, were employed on the 877 assembly lines at Gordon-Ganza Aviation in Long Beach, California."

The senators opened the files in front of them and saw the photos of the two Syrians. The pictures were the only items in the file that weren't complete fiction. The men's names weren't real and although they genuinely worked at Gordon-Ganza Aviation, they were recruited and employed by Blackthorn to do so. The men were both Syrian Americans and thought they were on a covert mission for the US government, installing vital surveillance equipment in commercial jets, unaware that they were actually being set up as fall guys for something much bigger.

"They both have familial ties to Harakat Ahrar al-Sham al-Islamiyya, the umbrella for multiple terrorists that are dedicated to establishing an Islamic state under strict Sharia law," Cross said. "The two men worked at Gordon-Ganza for one year before quitting their jobs and leaving the United States for Turkey. We believe they installed devices on two or more aircraft that allowed the autopilot system to be hacked by anyone with a wireless connection."

"Holy shit," Tolan said.

"You mentioned two aircraft," said Bradley Hazeltine, the honorable senator from North Carolina. "What is the other one?"

"We believe the Indonesian Air flight that went missing a year ago, which was also a Gordon-Ganza 877 manufactured while Darwish and Ebrahimi were working on the assembly line, was crashed in the first use of the device," Cross said. "A practice run, so to speak."

Healy spoke, trying to keep his voice flat and emotionless. He was furious at Cross on a personal level but, as acting director of the CIA, his priority was resolving this crisis. So, on that level, he was thankful for the intel, assuming it was solid. "What evidence do you have for the existence of this device?"

It was a fair question and Cross took it that way, answering Healy with a respectful, collegial tone.

"It began with something the captain said in the cockpit voice recording from the black box—"

Tolan interrupted him. "You got the recording?"

"The transcript is in your packet." Cross made the comment as if it were a minor detail but the intelligence acquisition was huge and represented another head shot to Healy's career. "The captain was convinced the plane was under the control of an outside party. He shut off all the computer systems to kill the autopilot, but not in time to save the plane."

Stowe closed the file and regarded Cross with undisguised disdain, though it looked more like he'd eaten a bad clam. "How did you get all of this information so fast and from so many sources?"

The senator knew the answer, and so did everybody else in the chamber, but Stowe wanted Cross' actions on the record, not that anyone was actually keeping one.

"We accessed the computers at Gordon-Ganza Aviation to obtain the names of all their employees and cross-referenced them against known members of terrorist groups," Cross answered without the slightest hesitation. "We also accessed US Customs, the NTSB, the TSA, and numerous other public and private databases."

"You mean you hacked them," Stowe said, as if Cross were feeding the senator a rancid meal that was making him sick. Healy understood the tone because he was feeling the same way. "What you did is illegal. Any evidence you acquired is tainted and inadmissible in court."

"This is not a case that will ever get to a courtroom. We both know that, Senator," Cross said. "This is about resolution and retribution."

"Damn straight," Holbrook said. "Where are these bastards now?"

"Belgium. They came across with a wave of Syrian refugees. We believe they are in a farmhouse outside of Antwerp."

In fact, he knew for certain that they were there. Both men were sedated and under guard by Blackthorn operatives who were staging the scene and stocking it with incriminating evidence as he was speaking.

Holbrook turned to Healy, who was trying to channel Mr. Spock and appear as objective and emotionless as he could, considering he was undergoing a political castration. "Can you get them?"

"Yes, Mr. Chairman," Healy said. "We'll coordinate with our Belgian counterparts and arrange—"

Holbrook cut him off with a wave of his hand and a scowl of disgust. He turned his head, and multiple chins, to Cross. "How quickly can your people do it?"

"Within the next three hours."

Holbrook shared glances with his fellow senators. They were all in silent agreement, even Stowe. He fixed his gaze back on Cross.

"Do it using your men but you've got to run the operation out of the CIA so there's no hint of private sector involvement. I'll clear it with the White House."

"That won't be a problem," Cross said and glanced at Healy, who nodded his consent, not that it mattered anymore.

CHAPTER TWENTY-TWO

Ian drove south on a flat stretch of Interstate 5 in Oregon that was bordered on both sides by dry, weed-strewn farmland, unmarked warehouses, and rusted mobile homes. Margo was asleep in the passenger seat, her head propped against the window, the jar of coins on the floor between her feet.

He liked the open road. There was something about driving, about putting his troubles in the rearview mirror and looking at a ribbon of asphalt stretching out into infinity in front of him, that cleared his head, bringing him peace and perspective. That was why whenever he was having problems in a relationship, or trouble plotting a story, he'd just get in his car and drive to San Francisco, Las Vegas, or Phoenix. He'd inevitably find the answer on the road. One of his girlfriends accused him of running away from his problems. (The truth was she resented her captive audience escaping during her most dramatic and overwrought performances.) But it was the opposite. He was running toward his problems, only from a different direction. This time, however, the girlfriend would have been right.

He'd killed a woman in Seattle in self-defense and he wanted to get as far from that corpse, and that memory, as he could. But escaping the people who'd sent her wouldn't be nearly as simple. At least he wouldn't have to run from the police, too. He was sure the CIA would clean up the crime scene for him, not to save him from prosecution, but to serve their selfish interests. They wouldn't want the body to lead back to them or to focus any law enforcement attention on him. The last thing they wanted was the police finding him before they did and Ian telling them what he knew, no matter how ridiculous his story would sound. So this was one instance where his interests and his enemy's were the same.

The Mustang hit a pothole. The bump jolted Margo awake and rattled the coins. She sat up, stretched, and rolled her head around to relieve her stiff neck. The first thing she noticed was the wretched stench from outside. That's why Ian had been breathing through his mouth for the last few miles.

"We must be passing through Millersburg," she said, "which is the best way to experience the town."

He knew she was right about where they were because he'd seen a road sign a while back but he didn't see anything along the road now that could qualify as a landmark.

"How do you know that's where we are?" he asked.

"It's known for smelling like a mountain of manure, though it's better since they closed the paper mill that used to be beside the freeway." She gestured out the window at the weed-choked foundations and parking lot that remained behind a chain-link fence. "They tore it down a few years back."

"So why does it still stink?"

"That's from the sewage treatment plant and the zirconium mining."

"Must be a lovely place to live," he said. "I guess the people get used to it after a while."

"Or everything smells and tastes like shit and they accept it as normal because that's the price they have to pay to live at all."

He gave her a look. "I'm guessing we're not talking about Millersburg anymore."

"All I signed on for was taking you around to a couple of bookstores," she said. "Now I've got killers after me. What the hell did I do to deserve this?"

"Nothing at all." Ian considered apologizing again but he didn't think that would make a difference.

"They're not going to stop because we killed that bitch last night," Margo said. "They're going to be even more pissed off. Next time they'll send four people like her, only armed with machine guns and hand grenades."

"They'll have to find us first."

"Where are we going?"

"We need to disappear. I have a friend who's been living off the grid for a while now. I'm hoping he can teach us how to do it."

"So that's it. We just run and hide."

He glanced at her. "Do you have a better idea?"

"Yeah, let's go to the FBI."

He didn't see how that was any less suicidal than going to the police but he decided to try a different argument. "And tell them what?"

"The CIA crashed that plane into Waikiki and it was your idea and now they want to kill you to cover it up."

"That sounds crazy," Ian said.

She turned in her seat to face him. "It's the story you told me and I believed it."

"Because you saw them try to kill me. You have evidence."

"There you go. We tell them how the CIA hacked a parked car and tried to—" She stopped, hearing her own words, which didn't sound believable even to her. "Okay, forget that. We tell them about the bitch who tried to kill us."

"The woman I impaled with a fireplace poker in the ransacked house where we stole this car."

"Yes," Margo said, then thought about it. "Okay, forget that, too. Just tell them the CIA part."

"I can't prove any of it," Ian said. "I don't even know the name of the guy who recruited me."

"What about those three dead writers? Doesn't that prove something?"

"I've got no evidence that they were murdered."

"They've tried three times to kill you."

"Or I'm accident-prone on top of having paranoid delusions," he said.

"So that's it. They win. We run and hide."

Ian nodded. "And we hope they never find us."

"That's no life."

"It's better than death," he said.

"Welcome to fucking Millersburg."

Langley, Virginia. July 19. 4:47 p.m. Eastern Standard Time.

The situation room at the Central Intelligence Agency wasn't nearly as high-tech as the one at Blackthorn's headquarters. The concept and general layout were the same but the equipment was older and placed in consoles that looked like they dated back to the Cold War. Where Blackthorn had a media wall, the CIA had a collection of monitors that reminded Cross of a sports bar.

He was greeted like an old friend by the agents in the room, their reaction falling just short of applause, probably because of the cold expression on Healy's face. Manning the command console was Norman Kelton, who'd been Cross' right hand for years but was too fiercely loyal to the agency to join him at Blackthorn. Now Kelton had his old job. Kelton never ran an operation without a pipe in his mouth and he had one today. Cross suspected that eating, drinking, and cunnilingus were the only things Kelton did without the pipe.

Kelton rose from his creaking leather office chair. "Hey, Will, did you come back for your chair?"

Cross shook his old friend's hand. "You can keep it, Norm."

Kelton gestured to the array of screens on the wall. "Your boys are in position and moving in."

The center screen displayed a satellite camera view that showed infrared images of several figures moving through a field toward a farmhouse from multiple directions. Two heat signatures were visible in the farmhouse. A satellite was the one toy that Blackthorn didn't have.

Healy was irritated by what he saw. "You had your people on the ground in Belgium before you walked into the Senate chamber."

"You say that like preparation is a bad thing," Cross said.

"Do the Belgians know anything about this operation?"

"We'll send them a fruit basket once we have Ayoub Darwish and Habib Ebrahimi under interrogation in our safe house in France." Cross didn't bother to disguise his irritation. He turned to Kelton. "Why aren't I seeing clear visuals from the helmet cams? It's just static."

"Bad uplink. Could be a hundred reasons for it," Kelton said. "But I'd bet it's because your high-end tech is incompatible with our Reagan-era satellites."

His bet was wrong. The reason was that the signal from the helmet cameras was being intentionally distorted at the source. Cross didn't want the CIA seeing anything clearly since the entire scene was staged. This was going to be a radio play accompanied by some entertaining graphics.

Being back here again, for the first time since he'd left several years ago, made him realize that he should've walked away from the CIA a lot sooner than he did. He'd stayed at the CIA through several presidential administrations, and the various agency directors, as an anonymous, essential cog in the machine because he loved the game of espionage and the global stakes. He believed that America's strength as a super-power depended on the decisions it made economically, militarily, and diplomatically. The success of those decisions depended on the quality of information gathered by the government's intelligence agencies.

There had always been big money to be made in corporate espionage or private security but he hadn't been interested. He'd overseen operations to topple governments, assassinate dictators, infiltrate foreign spy networks, kidnap terrorists, and sabotage enemy weapons systems. He couldn't get excited about protecting some high-flying CEO, stealing the recipe for Kentucky Fried Chicken, or sabotaging the launch of a new smartphone. The corporate stakes were mostly financial and rarely lethal. Nobody would kill for the design of the new Camry or die to keep it secret. So where was the fun or challenge in that?

But all that changed after 9/11. That was when the Pentagon began outsourcing some of their all-out war against terror to the private sector. Blackthorn had come to him then, dangling a big salary and stock options in front of him but he'd stayed at the CIA to fight for God and country. Then came the public backlash against the CIA's secret prisons, enhanced interrogation techniques, eavesdropping on Americans, and extraordinary renditions of terrorists from foreign soil. The aftermath brought budget cuts, increased operational and financial oversight from politicians, and the untenable demand that the agency respect the individual privacy of Americans and the sovereignty of other nations. The politicians were crippling the CIA and, by extension, endangering the country. That was when Cross decided to join Blackthorn. He saw an opportunity for Blackthorn in the restrictions being placed on the agency. Not just to make money, but to gain something much more valuable.

The old adage that "knowledge is power" had never been more accurate than it was today. Thanks to Cross, Blackthorn was on the cusp of controlling the nation's intelligence gathering. That meant that essentially Blackthorn would be deciding what the government knew about anything. And when that happened, not only would Cross be rich—he'd be pulling the strings on the president and, by extension, the US government, making them dance on the world stage any way he wanted.

A crackle came from the speakers, breaking into his thoughts, and was followed by a report from the ground team across the Atlantic.

OPERATIVE #1: We're going in.

The room was silent as the satellite view showed the ground team entering the farmhouse simultaneously through several entrances. At the same instant, a flash washed out the satellite screen and the sound of gunfire rattled the speakers.

"Shit," Kelton said, biting down on his pipe.

Everyone in the room was tense except for Healy, who, for an instant, smiled before catching himself and frowning. But Cross saw the smile out of the corner of his eye.

OPERATIVE #1: Tripwire. Explosive booby trap.
We are under fire. We are engaging the targets.

The gunfire abruptly ceased. The room was silent and filled with palpable apprehension. Cross leaned over the mike on Kelton's command console.

"Do you have the targets?" Cross asked.

OPERATIVE #1: Targets acquired.

"Any casualties?"

OPERATIVE #1: Both targets are down.

"Are their identities confirmed?"

OPERATIVE #1: Positive match.

Healy sighed. "There goes our chance to interrogate the suspects."

"It wasn't ever going to happen," Cross said. "They didn't want to be taken alive. We can get plenty of intel out of what they left behind, just like we did with bin Laden."

Cross faced the mike again. "Take everything—papers, books, computers, cell phones, and the bodies. Anything you can get your hands on."

OPERATIVE #1: Affirmative.

Kelton turned to one of his agents, who was seated at a nearby console and wearing headphones. "Any chatter about this on the Belgian police bands?"

The agent shook his head. "Not yet, sir. All quiet."

Kelton smiled at Cross. "Got to love bad guys who pick remote locations. Your boys might even have time to buy some Belgian chocolates for us on their way out of the country."

CHAPTER TWENTY-THREE

The Top A-1 Economy Motel was next door to a storage unit facility along a dusty, desolate portion of Highway 97 in Klamath Falls, Oregon. The only difference between the two one-story cinder-block structures was that the motel units had windows and doors instead of roll-up garage doors and it stored people instead of junk.

The rooms at the Top A-1 Economy Motel were only thirty-three dollars a night so it was popular with truckers, adulterers, runaways, day laborers, and drunks. Only one room was vacant when Ian and Margo showed up and it had a table with two chairs, an old TV, a microwave on top of a four-drawer dresser, and a queen-size bed with a vinyl-padded headboard bolted into the wall.

"It's not the Four Seasons," Ian said as they came in carrying their suitcases. "But it'll do as a place to rest up until tomorrow morning."

"We've still got a few hours of daylight left. I don't see why we're stopping now." She clutched the jar of coins like it was a treasure chest.

"Because we've been driving for seven and a half hours," Ian said, closing the door. "And that also happens to be how many hours of sleep I've had over the last two days. I'm exhausted and I need to rest."

"Fine. You sleep and I'll drive. Just give me the directions to wherever we're going."

"It's not that easy. I know my way by sight, not highways or street names and I don't want to make the drive in the dark. We'll leave first thing in the morning." He set the suitcase by the door, sat down on the bed, and fell back onto it. "Oh, that feels nice."

Actually, he could feel every spring in the saggy mattress, but he was exhausted, and lying anywhere, even on a sidewalk, would have felt good to him right now.

Margo hadn't moved from where she stood. "I'm a lesbian."

"Okay," Ian said.

"I moved to Seattle from Walla Walla with my lover and six months after we got there she left me for another woman."

"I'm sorry to hear that."

"You mean that I'm not straight."

"I mean that you got your heart broken."

"I've broken plenty of hearts myself," she said, then quickly added, "all of them women. I'm not into dicks at all."

"I believe you. You're as lesbian as it gets."

"Just so we're clear," she said.

"All I want to do in this bed is sleep, Margo. I'm not going to make a move on you if that's what you're worried about."

She set the jar of coins down on the table. "I'm not."

"Then why are you telling me that you're a lesbian?"

"Because you're talking about a life on the run together, at least for a while, and if you thought it might someday turn into a thing, I want you to know that it's not going to happen. Ever."

"The romantic possibilities of this situation never crossed my mind."

"There are no romantic possibilities. *That's* what I'm saying."

"Understood," Ian said.

"Good," she said.

"But now that you mention it, James Bond got Pussy Galore to switch sides."

"You're not James Bond." Margo trudged to the bathroom and closed the door.

"Thanks for reminding me," Ian said to himself and closed his eyes.

⊕

While he was sleeping, she took the car and came back with a bucket of Kentucky Fried Chicken, four buttermilk biscuits, and a couple of Cokes. The smell of the chicken woke him up and eating it out of the bucket was almost as good as sex. He didn't realize how hungry he was or how satisfying fried chicken could be. After their meal, they sat side by side in bed together, greasy-fingered and sated, and watched one of the *Star Trek* movies that starred the geriatric, overweight cast from the original TV series. Ian was shirtless and in boxers and she was wearing a T-shirt and panties. It would have been a dream date, if only they weren't running for their lives from the CIA and she wasn't a lesbian.

"Do you have anyone in your life?" Margo asked.

"You mean like a wife or a girlfriend?"

"Yeah."

"Why do you ask?" It certainly wasn't because seeing him in his boxers made her horny. She'd made that very clear.

"Because you're ready to go into hiding for God knows how long but you don't seem concerned about the life, or the people, that you're leaving behind."

She was looking at their situation in ways that hadn't occurred to him. First, she'd considered what running off together might mean relationship-wise for the two of them and now she was wondering what the emotional cost might be. He was more focused on basic survival. But she deserved to have her questions answered.

"I've never been married. I've had a few serious relationships, nothing that's lasted longer than a couple of years," he said. "I've always been too focused on my career, or too lost in my stories, or so my exes have told me. But it was the same for them, too. They were always chasing the next role."

"So you only date actresses?"

"Every woman in LA is an actress or model," Ian said. "Or waiting to be discovered as one."

"That's such a cliché," she said.

"You've obviously never spent much time in LA."

"Do you have a family?"

"I'm an only child. My father was a newspaper reporter in LA. My mom went to parties for a living, covering the society beat. They divorced when I was a kid. He died ten years ago. He was an editor for a small-town newspaper in the Midwest. She's down in Palm Springs, still going to parties, and hoping to marry a rich plastic surgeon so she can save some money on all the work she's having done. You?"

"I'm single. My parents have been married for thirty-five years and have lived in the same house in Walla Walla, Washington, for all of them. My dad sells insurance through his own agency and my older brother works for him. I was supposed to work there, too, until I found a good husband and raised kids."

"You don't strike me as an insurance salesman," Ian said, stealing a glance at her pierced belly button. It hurt just to look at the silver stud. "Or a housewife."

"You see that clearly but my family didn't," she said. "Not until I brought a girl from Milton-Freewater as my date to the prom. They still haven't gotten over the shock of it or accepted who I am."

"Who are you?" Ian asked.

She cocked her head, studying his face. "I thought we discussed that."

"You're more than who you like to fuck. I'm talking about what you want to do, what you're passionate about. I assume your dream isn't dog sitting and driving asshole writers around."

"I'm a struggling singer-songwriter," she said. "I play in a few bars and coffeehouses in Seattle but I haven't had much success. None, actually."

"What kind of singer are you?"

She thought about that for a moment. "Imagine Nina Simone crossed with Joni Mitchell singing about doomed lesbian love and Walla Walla sweet onions."

"Isn't there enough of that out there already?"

She laughed. "Careful, Ian, I might start to like you."

He smiled. It felt good to make her laugh. "Enough to switch teams?"

"Not that much," she said.

They watched another *Star Trek* movie, marveled at William Shatner's toupee and girdle, then fell asleep in bed together, their bodies never touching.

An Excerpt from *Death Is the Beginning* by Ian Ludlow

Straker's mastery of the ancient erotic art of 性的超越, or *Seiteki chōetsu*, kept KGB agent Ivanka Anasenko on the verge of a full-body, deep-tissue, nerve-shattering orgasm for three straight hours. Her pale skin was dappled with sweat and almost every muscle in her body, from her eyelids to her curled toes, was as taut as piano wire, ready to be released in glorious spasms of ecstasy with just the right touch. He played her body like an instrument, her moans and quivers the musical notes. It was his favorite tune.

Some disciples of *Seiteki chōetsu* stroked the skin and genitals of their lovers with razors or knives instead of their fingers or tongues but Straker considered that showing off. Besides, Anasenko would have never let him near her naked body with such obvious weapons.

Now he was playing her with another part of his anatomy, each thrust a balletic exploration of her inner woman that made her entire face tremble with ecstasy. He thought about those Cialis ads on TV, warning men to call a doctor for an erection lasting longer than four hours. The ads always amused him. If he couldn't stay hard for eight hours, it wasn't worth getting up. But tonight was different. He didn't have the time to spare to adequately satisfy himself.

"Now," she begged him. "Please."

Ivanka Anasenko was physically fit, supremely so, but he knew she didn't have the stamina for full *Seiteki chōetsu*. The only woman he'd ever known who did was the one who'd taught him the ancient art. But Anasenko had endured longer than most women could.

"Are you sure?" he whispered into her ear. Even his words, the feel of his breath on her ear, made her eyelids quiver with desire. The right pitch of his voice would be enough to push her over the edge, but not enough to accomplish his goal.

"God, yes," she said but it sounded more like a moan.

He slowly pulled out of her, making her body shudder, and sat on the edge of the bed, studying her. This pause, too, was part of the technique and perhaps its most exquisite expression. She was beautiful in this state of transcendent arousal. He could almost forget that she was an enemy agent and a coldhearted killer.

"You can't leave me like this," she whispered imploringly, as if she were tied naked to the rack rather than lying unbound on her bed, her body frozen with erotic tension and aching, bone-deep lust.

He flicked one of her hard nipples like a light switch. She instantly began convulsing as one powerful orgasm after another roiled through her body, her eyes rolling back in her head as she endured the mind-blowing pleasure.

Straker stood and dressed, paying little attention to her ecstasy, until she finally slipped into unconsciousness. He tied his shoes and then checked her pulse, just to be sure he hadn't accidentally killed her. Deaths often occurred when amateurs attempted *Seiteki chōetsu*, even without knives. It had never happened to him, of course, but he couldn't be certain she didn't have a family history of congenital heart defects that wasn't noted in her file. Her pulse was healthy. She was still alive but he was certain that she wouldn't regain consciousness for hours, perhaps days.

That gave him more than enough time to break into the Kremlin, steal the Miernik dossier, and still make it to Pamplona tomorrow to run with the bulls.

CHAPTER TWENTY-FOUR

Klamath Falls, Oregon. July 20. 7:07 a.m. Pacific Standard Time.

The Walmart had just opened and there were more employees in the store than customers. The aisles were virtually deserted. Ian and Margo moved down the snack food aisle, Ian filling their cart with bags of chips and cookies on the go without giving any attention to what he was grabbing. She was dismayed by his choices.

"I thought we were trying to stay alive," Margo said, picking up a bag of pork rinds as an example. "This stuff will kill us before the CIA can."

"It's not for us. It's for Ronnie."

"Who's Ronnie?" She dropped the pork rinds back into the cart and absently wiped her hand on her pant leg to remove grease that wasn't there.

"He's the guy we're on our way to see," Ian said. "He rarely ventures out and he loves junk food."

Ian wheeled the cart to the self-serve checkout station. He wasn't worried about being seen on security cameras. He doubted that the CIA could monitor every camera in every store in America for their faces, but he didn't want to spend time with a cashier. They were paying with cash, and they weren't wanted felons, so the odds of anybody coming along later and asking about them were slim. Even so, he still thought it was better to avoid giving anyone much of an opportunity to see and remember them. The cashier probably didn't see many people with duct-taped casts on their arms.

Ian scanned the items over the bar-code reader while Margo bagged them.

"How far do we have to go?" she asked.

"A few more hours."

"How long has it been since you saw him?"

"About five years, right after he left LA for Nevada to live off the grid," Ian said, passing some Ho Hos and Ding Dongs over the scanner. "I went out and tried to talk him into coming back but it didn't work."

"Why did he exile himself?"

Ian sighed. "To escape constant government surveillance and to survive the man-made pandemic that the global elites will unleash to exterminate fifty percent of the world's population so they can keep earth's limited resources for themselves."

"Oh, that," Margo said. "Now that you've given me the executive summary, let's hear the details."

He didn't want to go into the details because he knew how it would sound but there was no way to avoid it. "It goes back to 9/11."

"Of course it does," she said.

That was the reaction he was afraid of. He fed some bills into the machine and pocketed the change, and Margo pushed the cart to the door. Usually at Walmart, a retiree in a blue vest was posted at the door to double-check customer receipts against whatever was in the cart. But there was no old fogey there this morning. So they simply walked between the two hard plastic security panels that scanned them for shoplifted items and then they went out the door to the parking lot.

Ian resumed his explanation as they walked to the car. "Ronnie believes that our government knew the attack on the World Trade Center was coming, and either instigated it or smoothed the way for it to happen, to get the country behind the invasion of Afghanistan and the Second Gulf War."

"Why would they want to do that?"

Ian opened the trunk and they began loading the groceries inside. "The global elites control the government and own the military-industrial complex so the war kept them rich and funded the production of the weaponry they'd need for world domination. It also led to the creation of the Patriot Act, which granted the government enormous and unprecedented surveillance and warrantless search-and-seizure powers."

Ian closed the trunk, walked around to the driver's side of the car, and got in. He waited until Margo got into her seat to continue his explanation. "There was political opposition to the Patriot Act because it was a blatant rights grab but that disappeared after anthrax was mailed to some senators, making terrorism personal for them. The anthrax scare was perpetrated by the government, of course, to generate the popular and political support to get the act passed. Ronnie believes the true purpose of the law was to give the government, which is controlled by the global elites, the power to identify opposition and squash dissent among the American people."

"Uh-huh," Margo said. "And what's the point of all these devious machinations?"

"The world has limited natural resources—food, water, land, fossil fuels—all of which are already seriously endangered by population growth and it's only getting worse. And that's not even factoring in the pollution and global warming created by an ever-increasing global population." Ian put on his seat belt, started the car, and drove out of the parking lot, all with only his left hand, which made the simple tasks difficult. "The global elites want to keep it all for themselves so they've not only got to stop the population growth but also reduce the current demand for those resources."

"That's where the global pandemic comes in," Margo said. "Some superbug that kills everybody who hasn't been secretly vaccinated."

"Yes, but to set the stage, over the last decade or so a startling number of top microbiologists worldwide have been dying in accidents and by natural causes at a rate that Ronnie believes is far above normal, according to actuarial tables. That was done to get rid of anybody with the ability to stop the global pandemic that only the elites, and their chosen followers, will survive."

"Why was the government spying on your friend?"

"They're spying on all of us but giving him extra scrutiny because he knew what they were doing and was warning others on secret message boards on the dark web. They started following him, reading his e-mails, listening to his calls, drugging his food, and messing with his head. So, to save himself and his sanity, he fled Los Angeles and got completely off the grid. He couldn't stop them from pulling off their global pandemic or whatever apocalyptic event they created but he was determined to survive it. That would be his rebellion."

Ian drove onto the highway heading southeast and waited for Margo's reaction. She was silent for a few moments before she spoke.

"The bottom line is that we're driving hundreds of miles to seek the advice of a crazy survivalist preparing for the zombie apocalypse."

"I didn't say anything about zombies."

"But you aren't disputing that he's crazy."

Ian chose his words carefully. "He has an unusual worldview but he also has the vital skills we need to learn if we want to survive."

"The zombie apocalypse," she said.

"The rest of the week," he said.

CHAPTER TWENTY-FIVE

Cross was in a conference room, briefing the three owners and founders of Blackthorn Global Security about the status of his "outside efforts," as he quaintly characterized them, to exert pressure on the government to accept their proposal to privatize most of the CIA's covert operations business. Not that it was a business yet, but it would be soon, and an extraordinarily lucrative one, if everything worked out as he'd planned. And so far, with the exception of a minor hitch with Ian Ludlow, it was. He left that hitch out of his briefing to the three owners—an oil company magnate, the leader of a major bank, and a former US vice president who had a significant stake in a major defense contractor.

"The bodies of Ayoub Darwish and Habib Ebrahimi and their computers will be arriving here in the morning," Cross said, concluding the substance of his briefing. "We'll be taking the lead on the autopsies and analysis of the devices recovered from the farmhouse."

"Excellent work, Wilton," the oilman said. "Where does the success of this operation leave us on the outsourcing proposal?"

"Senator Holbrook went straight to the Oval Office to convey to the president the committee's unanimous recommendation. I'm confident the president will sign a classified executive order within forty-eight hours outsourcing the majority of the agency's covert operations to us . . . under the guise of a standard 'administrative and management support' contract. The president was a businessman himself. He's always believed the private sector can do a better job than government."

"What does Mike Healy think?" asked the former vice president.

"He thinks his balls have been cut off and served to us on a silver platter."

Everyone smiled. It was a good day. Cross looked out the glass partition and saw Victoria coming his way from the situation room.

"How much do you think we can expect to earn annually from this contract?" The banker could always be counted on to ask about the money.

"Conservatively? One billion dollars," Cross said.

Victoria paused outside the door and met his eye. He nodded, giving her consent to enter. She came in, gave an airline hostess smile to each of the men, and stepped up close to Cross, speaking quietly into his ear. "Sir, could I have a word? It's urgent."

"Excuse me, gentlemen," Cross said. "I have a small operational matter to deal with. It will just be a moment."

He stepped out of the conference room with her and then down the hall, where the three billionaires couldn't see them and read their facial expressions or body language. The men weren't fools.

She spoke as soon as they were out of sight. "We got a hit on Ian Ludlow and Margo French from a Walmart in Klamath Falls, Oregon."

That didn't make sense. Ludlow and French were dead. "What kind of hit?"

"The radio-frequency ID chips in their driver's licenses pinged the 'known shoplifter' profiles that we planted for Ludlow and French in all of the national chain-store security databases after they first eluded us in Seattle."

Several explanations came to his mind. One was that the hit was a false positive from a software glitch or it was a mechanical error. Another possibility was that someone stole the wallets from Ludlow and French before they got to the house, or after they were killed, which meant there was another loose end with a heartbeat that had to be tracked down. The third was that Ludlow and French were in Klamath Falls, which would be hard for them to do, unless their ghosts went shopping.

"Do you think it's a software glitch or a mechanical one?" he asked.

"Both are conceivable explanations but also highly unlikely. I could see one false positive at a location, but not two at the same time."

"Do we have photos from the store?"

"No," she said. "The purchases were made right when the store opened. The camera system was being rebooted and backed up at the time."

"Have you followed up with the asset? Did Ludlow and French have their IDs on them before they were killed?"

Victoria shifted her weight, telegraphing her discomfort. "I haven't been able to reach her."

Cross didn't like this. "You've had no contact with the asset since she confirmed the kill last night?"

Victoria nodded.

This was unsettling news. The asset's behavior was highly irregular. Assets were always reachable unless they were on a flight or were in the middle of executing a kill—or were dead.

"Where is the asset supposed to be right now?" he asked.

"Awaiting instructions in Seattle. I kept her there in case we learned that French shared whatever information she got from Ludlow with a third party."

The implication being that more killings might be necessary. Cross thought it was a wise precaution on Victoria's part to keep the asset in Seattle after the kill but it made the subsequent silence even more disturbing.

"Trigger the intruder alarm at the house in Seattle. Let's see what the police discover." He thought for a moment. The driver's licenses weren't the only things that had RFID chips in them. These days almost everything did, from breakfast cereal boxes to key chains. "Do you have the RFIDs from the products that Ludlow and French bought at Walmart?"

"It's all junk food."

"I don't care what it is as long as there are RFID chips in the packaging that we can home in on," he said. "Get our combat drone at Nellis Air Force Base airborne and searching for any combination of those RFIDs around Klamath Falls."

She nodded and headed back to the situation room. It was a large search area and the odds of the drone happening upon those RFIDs were slim. They needed to find a way to narrow the possible location of their targets, whoever they were.

Cross took a deep breath. He couldn't let any sign of problems creep into his expression, his gait, or his tone of voice. It conveyed vulnerability and weakness, something his bosses were instinctively attracted to, like blood in the water to sharks. He waited until he was sure he was in complete control of himself, then returned to the conference room to tell his masters what they wanted to hear.

CHAPTER TWENTY-SIX

At the Nevada state line, the two-lane strip of highway through the vacant grasslands abruptly became an unpaved dirt-and-gravel road that stretched out over a low rise and then down into a long valley. A twisted and peeling roadside sign riddled with bullet holes announced that Ian and Margo were entering Washoe County, Nevada, that the road was not maintained, and that they were traveling at their own risk. As if that weren't enough to dissuade them from venturing on, ahead were uninhabited places like Massacre Lake and Hell Creek, all named to underscore that this was a landscape more hospitable to death than a long, healthy life.

The old Mustang wasn't built for rutted dirt roads so their journey wasn't a pleasant one, the car bumping and rocking along as they delved deeper into the desolate expanse of rocks and sagebrush. Far across the dry valley, they could see the serrated edge of a long, barren mountain range that had doomed many settlers heading for Oregon.

Ian and Margo passed through Vya, a ghost town of three decrepit wooden buildings, but after that, they didn't see any more structures. They also didn't see any other vehicles or human beings. They were seemingly alone in the middle of a vast nowhere. Ian felt conflicting emotions: relief, because he was far away from civilization and all the spying technology that went along with it, and vulnerability, because he was completely out in the open, easy to spot and kill if anyone knew where to look. But he was fairly certain that nobody did.

Ian recognized some landmarks along the way from his last trip out here—a rock formation that resembled a skull, a dry lake bed with some bones scattered across it, and the rotting hulk of an old truck—that helped him know when to turn off one dirt road and down another. Eventually, he drove through a cleft between two rocky hills, what Ronnie called "Mother Nature's Glorious Cleavage," into a hidden clearing where a ramshackle compound had been built.

A cinder-block house with barred windows and an array of solar panels on the roof was at the center of the compound. Radiating out from the house were a greenhouse, a utility shed, a corral with goats, chickens, cows, and a surprisingly lush vegetable garden. A bulldozer, a tractor, and a pickup truck were scattered around like a child's forgotten toys. There was a gasoline pump and tanks for water and propane. So while it was clear that somebody was living there, nobody was in sight. The air was still and it was eerily quiet.

Ian parked in front of the house and turned to Margo. "I'm sure that he saw us coming for miles and he doesn't know who we are. Get out slowly with your hands in the air. We don't want to get shot."

"This is starting out well," she said.

Ian got out of the car, his arms raised, which wasn't easy with one arm in a cast. Margo got out with her arms up, too, looking around for signs of life besides the listless livestock.

"Ronnie," Ian shouted. "It's Ian Ludlow and a friend. We've come with Doritos."

"Doritos!" Ronnie shouted back excitedly from one of the hills. "Hot damn. What else have you got?"

Ian lowered his hands and popped the trunk so he could survey the bounty of goods. "Cheetos. Cap'n Crunch. Oreos. Funyuns. Pop-Tarts. Pork rinds."

"All the essential food groups," Ronnie said, much closer this time.

Margo turned toward the rocks. She saw a man but was momentarily blinded by the sunshine reflecting off his aluminum foil–wrapped soldier's helmet. When her vision cleared, she saw the aluminum helmet was atop a deeply tanned, heavily bearded, potbellied man in his forties wearing Ray-Ban Wayfarers and a sweat-stained camouflage tank top and pants, and carrying a rocket-propelled grenade launcher.

She stared at him, her head cocked. Ian could read her expression. Something was familiar to her about this strange man but she couldn't quite put her finger on it.

Ronnie dropped the grenade launcher on the hood of the Mustang and embraced Ian in a bear hug. Ian wasn't an affectionate man by nature but it felt good, after everything they'd been through, to be in the strong embrace of someone who cared about him.

"Long time, man," Ronnie said. "Way too long."

They stepped apart, all smiles, and appraised each other.

"You're looking good," Ian said.

"Masturbation. Three to six times daily. That's the key," Ronnie said. "But you know that. You're a writer."

"I did not know that," Ian said.

"That explains why you look like you've been constipated for a month."

"That's not why but we'll get to that in a minute." Ian looked past his friend to Margo. "Ronnie, this is Margo French. Margo, this is—"

She interrupted him, because now she knew the answer and it pissed her off.

"The Vine. Ronnie Mancuso," she said. "*The fucking Vine.*"

The last three words were hissed like an accusation and pointed at Ian.

"Half-man, half-plant, all cop. That's me." Ronnie puffed out his chest with pride. "Not only did it pay for all this"—he swept his arm in front of him, gesturing to his kingdom—"but I've been able to communicate with plants ever since. Nothing would have grown here otherwise."

"No, no, no." Margo shook her head and fell back against the car. "This isn't happening."

Ronnie smiled at Ian. "Wow. My star power hasn't dimmed. It's blinding, man. Another reason I had to go where I couldn't be seen." He turned to Margo. "Yes, it's me. I know it's thrilling but get over it, darling. I crap just like you do. Maybe more."

But she wasn't looking at him. Her furious gaze was fixed on Ian. "I can't believe you dragged me out here. *This* guy is your Yoda? The fucking Vine? If I have to become him to survive, the CIA can kill me now."

Ronnie jerked as if electrocuted. "The C-I-A?"

Margo had spoken the three letters that were certain to get Ronnie's full attention. Maybe it was Ian's imagination but it looked like Ronnie's ears had perked up like a dog's.

"Have you heard about the plane crash in Honolulu?" Ian asked.

"Of course," Ronnie said. "I have a radio. I need to stay on top of current events to know when the End of Days is coming."

Ronnie's mention of the End of Days drew a derisive groan from Margo. Ian ignored it and pressed on.

"The crash was a terrorism scenario I came up with for the CIA to help the government prepare for the worst," Ian said. "But the CIA went out and did it. They crashed the plane. I don't know why they did it. But now they want me dead and Margo dead, too."

Ronnie walked past Ian and regarded the Walmart bags in the trunk as if they were rattlesnakes. "How long ago were you at Walmart?"

"About four hours," Ian said but he quickly reassured his friend. "It's okay, we paid cash. We know not to use our credit cards ever again."

"It doesn't matter. You're toast." Ronnie slammed the trunk closed and marched to the corral, a man on a mission.

"What are you talking about?" Ian asked.

"Every product Walmart sells is embedded with a radio-frequency ID chip, either in the item itself or in the packaging so they can track their inventory globally. If you don't think the government is watching that, too, you're delusional."

"That's funny coming from you, especially after what you just said." Margo turned to Ian. "Can we go now?"

"No." Ian headed to the corral, where Ronnie was putting ropes around the necks of three goats. He needed to understand how he'd screwed up and the full scope and consequences of his mistake. "Okay, so they know when a box of Oreos leaves the store. How does that point anybody to us?"

Ronnie replied as he led the three goats out of the corral. "You think groceries, books, and other products are the only things with RFID tags? Your driver's license and credit cards all have them, too. We're all just inventory being tracked by the New World Order, man. Do you know why I wear a helmet wrapped with aluminum foil?"

Margo spoke up. "Because you're a lunatic."

"To block the signal from the RFID chip in my body, honey." Ronnie led the goats to his house, opened the front door, then let the animals loose inside.

"Of course," Margo said, then turned to Ian. "I just want to point out that we're talking to a man who wraps his head in aluminum foil and lives in a house with his goats."

Ronnie closed the door to the house, marched up to Margo, and held out his hand to her. "Give me your credit cards."

"Why would I do that?" she asked.

"Haven't you listened to a word I've said? They have RFID chips in them that can identify and pinpoint you."

She glanced at Ian. He shrugged and said, "We can't use them again anyway."

"Fine." Margo opened the car door and dug around in her purse. "You can decorate your hat with them and make a real fashion statement."

Ian reached into his pocket, pulled his credit cards out of his wallet, and handed them to Ronnie. "Here you go. How do you think RFID chips got into your body?"

"I don't know *when* they put one in but I know it's *there*."

"Because you hear voices." Margo gave Ronnie her credit cards and slung her purse strap over her shoulder.

"Of course not," Ronnie said. "That would be crazy."

"Look who's talking," Margo said.

"RFID chips don't transmit audio or video. They share data," Ronnie said. "I know I've got one because the government followed me everywhere until I blocked their signal. Now they don't know where I am. You're the first people to come out here in years. The odds are fifty-fifty that you've got chips in you, too. They're putting the chips in *everybody*."

"I'd notice if someone surgically implanted a chip in me," Margo said.

"No, you wouldn't. The RFID chips they use now are smaller than a grain of sand," Ronnie said. "The New World Order began by testing them on our pets and we all gladly played along. Once they refined their technology with our dogs and cats and proved that it worked, they miniaturized the chips even further. They began secretly implanting the chips in us whenever we had surgery and then through flu vaccines. Why do you think they make the shots so cheap or even free?"

"Why would they want to track people?" she asked.

"You know what cancer is? It's mass multiplication of deadly cells. That's what the global elites think that people are becoming to planet Earth. Soon there won't be enough resources to feed everybody, let alone for the special few, the global elites, to prosper." Ronnie marched back to the house, opened the door, tossed the credit cards inside, and closed the door again. "So they need to cut the population in half and kill anybody they can't control or who doesn't measure up to their physical and intellectual standards for the master race."

Margo looked at Ian and spun a finger beside the side of her head to illustrate what she thought of Ronnie's theories. But Ian didn't see it that way. He was terrified. The conspiracy theories weren't what scared him. They were a distraction. It was the simple, terrifying point at the heart of everything that Ronnie said that made him tremble.

"The CIA knows we're here," Ian said.

"Hell yes. Winter is coming." Ronnie came back to the Mustang, grabbed the RPG launcher off the hood, and headed out into the field toward some boulders.

"He is batshit crazy," Margo said.

Ian disagreed. He trusted what his heart was telling him. He was a fool to think he'd outsmarted the CIA. The only thing that had kept them alive this long was pure, dumb luck and it may have just run out.

Ronnie crouched beside a boulder and lifted it up with one hand. It was an astonishing feat and it took Ian an instant to realize the boulder was fake and that it hid a hatch. From where he stood, Ian could see that under the hatch was a concrete staircase leading underground.

Ronnie waved them over. "Come with me if you want to live."

CHAPTER TWENTY-SEVEN

"Oh no," Margo said. "I am not going into an underground bunker with an insane chronic masturbator."

"Do you have a better idea?" Ian asked.

"That is not a reasonable basis for making decisions."

"It's all I've got." He tossed her the car keys and she caught them. "Thank you for everything. I wouldn't have survived this long without you. I hope you make it."

Ian walked to the hatch, feeling her eyes on his back. He knew what she was thinking because he'd thought it himself. If she didn't go into the bunker, she'd be on her own, running from assassins, with nowhere to go and only a jar of coins to fund her journey. It wasn't a great alternative to the one that Ronnie offered.

"I'm done being an author escort," Margo said in frustration and caught up to him as he reached the opening to the bunker. She held the keys out to him.

"You can keep them," Ian said. "I'm not going anywhere without you, not until I know you'll be safe."

She smiled and he thought he saw genuine warmth behind it. "You better not, or I'll kill you myself. You're the reason I'm in this fucking mess."

She dropped the keys in her purse. Ian went down the steps first, Margo right behind him. Ronnie brought up the rear, closing the hatch behind them. LED lights automatically switched on, illuminating a heavy steel door at the bottom of the stairs. It looked like the entrance to a bank vault. Ronnie knocked on it. The door sounded thick.

"This is an airtight, military-grade blast door. Nothing can get through it, not man nor microbe." Ronnie typed a code into a keypad on the wall. There was a loud clank as a bolt retracted inside the door. He spun the hatch wheel, pulled the thick door open, and ushered them in with a sweep of his arm. "Welcome to my home away from home."

The bunker was tubular, with white corrugated-metal walls. It looked to Ian like they were stepping into a buried submarine that had been furnished like a motor home. The first space was a family room with hardwood floors and rugs. A leather couch and matching recliners faced a flat-screen TV mounted on a stacked stone wall that added a rustic touch. Ian had a strong sense of déjà vu even though he'd never been in an underground bunker before.

The family room opened onto a kitchen with high-end appliances, oak cabinetry, granite countertops, a subway-tile backsplash, and a built-in dining table with upholstered bench seats. At the far end of the kitchen, a watertight door with a hatch wheel led to more rooms beyond.

"I hate to admit it," Margo said, "but this is pretty cool."

Ian realized why it looked familiar and turned to Ronnie. "Isn't this the same interior as your trailer on *Hollywood & the Vine*?"

"Yes, it is. That's when I first started designing this. Interior design isn't one of my gifts but I knew I liked my trailer." Ronnie pulled the heavy door closed, spinning the hatch wheel to lock it. "The shelter is seventy-five feet long, constructed of high-gauge steel encased in concrete and buried twenty feet below the ground. It's fully self-contained—safe from nuclear fallout, chemical attack, or biological warfare—and stocked with enough supplies to sustain four people for five years or one person for two decades."

Ian couldn't imagine spending five days locked in here without seeing daylight. Five years would be unbearable.

"Was this a submarine?" Ian asked.

"Nope, but it has a lot in common with one," Ronnie said. "All it's missing are the engine, propellers, and torpedoes."

"Where's the periscope?"

"Right here, smart-ass." Ronnie flicked a switch on the wall and the flat-screen monitor came on. The high-definition image was broken into quarters and showed the compound above from four angles, two from high cameras hidden in the hills.

"These are only some of my cameras. I've got complete surveillance of my domain. We'll know if a jackrabbit shows up." Ronnie went into the kitchen, opened a drawer, and put a roll of aluminum foil on the counter. "Wrap your driver's licenses with this."

"Okeydoke" Margo said, digging her license out of her purse. "But I draw the line at wrapping my head with it."

"Me too," Ian said.

"We'll see," Ronnie said.

That sounded ominous to Ian, but not as scary as facing more CIA assassins. Ian and Margo each took a strip of foil and wrapped their licenses.

CHAPTER TWENTY-EIGHT

Reseda, California. Eight Years Ago.

EXT. FOREST—DAY

Hollywood and Vine, their guns drawn and wearing
Kevlar vests, move cautiously through the trees.
Hollywood goes from tree to tree, using them for
cover but Vine is walking out in the open. This
frustrates Hollywood.

> HOLLYWOOD
> There are two neo-Nazi killers some-
> where in these woods with the loot they
> robbed from CalNorth Bank.

> VINE
> I know why we're here.

                    HOLLYWOOD
Then what the hell are you doing stroll-
ing out in the open? You might as well
have a target painted on your chest.

                      VINE
What am I supposed to do?

                    HOLLYWOOD
Use the trees for cover.

                      VINE
Would you use your sister for cover?

Hollywood gestures to the tree beside Vine.

                    HOLLYWOOD
That is not your sister.

                      VINE
No, it's not. It's a distant cousin.

Suddenly gunshots ring out from the forest ahead.
Hollywood takes cover behind a tree . . . and Vine
leaps in front of it, TAKING THE BULLETS that would
have slammed into the trunk. Vine goes down, his
gun flying out of his hand.

                    HOLLYWOOD
    Vine!

Furious, Hollywood picks up Vine's gun and, with a weapon in each hand, charges out into the open, guns blazing. He takes down both Nazis, then hurries back to his fallen partner.

Hollywood crouches beside Vine . . . who has taken two bullets in the center of his vest. Vine got the wind knocked out of him but otherwise he's fine.

                    HOLLYWOOD (CONT'D)
    Tell me you didn't just take a bullet
    for a tree.

                        VINE
    Two. Bullets.

                    HOLLYWOOD
    That was the dumbest thing I've ever
    seen a cop do.

It was certainly the dumbest thing that Ian had ever written. He hated himself as he was writing it but if he didn't get this script done today, then two hundred crew members of *Hollywood & the Vine* would be sitting around on Monday with nothing to shoot, the series would go on hiatus until new scripts were ready, and he'd never work in television again. He felt that pressure like a vise, squeezing his head, forcing the crap out of his imagination and onto his computer screen.

He was hunched over his laptop in his windowless office in a warehouse in Reseda that had been converted into a soundstage. The production designer had taken pity on Ian and built him a fake window, with a picture of San Francisco Bay, and installed it on one of his cinder-block walls so it felt less like he was writing his prison memoirs in solitary confinement.

Ian stared at the Golden Gate Bridge and, his head pounding, tried to think of a comeback line for Vine that wouldn't get his Writers Guild membership card revoked for gross negligence. He typed:

```
                    VINE
      But  I  bet  you've  never  seen  another
      cop bloom in the  spring, either.
```

The line was terrible. The script was terrible. The whole fucking show was terrible. He was a TV writer, living the dream he had when he was a kid. But nobody told him the dream came with fine print: *You'll be writing for a plant that fights crime.*

He also got none of the prestige that came from being a TV writer. Nobody was clamoring to hire him, and not even aspiring actresses, who were attracted to just about any producer on any series, were impressed by the credit. He needed to get on a tiffany show, something with miserable but beautiful doctors in constant angst, or conflicted but beautiful lawyers in perfectly tailored suits eloquently arguing about social issues. Those were shows that would get him respect and, more important, fucked by lots of actresses.

There was an urgent knock at his half-open door and then an assistant director poked his head into the room. The ADs were easy to spot. They all wore earpieces that kept them in radio communication with the rest of the crew and they were perpetually in a rush, as if they were doomed to always be hurrying to catch a departing train.

"We need you on the set," the AD said. "We've got a big problem."

"I'm writing. Couldn't you tell from the gun I had in my mouth when you walked in?"

The AD gave him a blank look. "I don't see a gun."

That was another thing that made ADs easy to spot: They had no sense of humor. That was what happened when you lived in constant crisis. "Grab another producer, preferably one of the guys who has a real window in his office."

"I would but it's Ronnie. He's in one of his moods and he won't come to the set."

Everyone knew that Ian was the only producer who could talk to Ronnie when the actor was in what they called "one of his moods." It was nicer than saying "psychotic break," "nervous breakdown," "panic attack," or "crazy tantrums." Those were phrases that, if heard by the wrong people, could make the actor uninsurable and could lead to the series being shut down or canceled. As appealing as that possibility was to Ian at that moment, he felt an obligation to the crew. They had mortgages to pay and kids to put through school. All he had over his head was a lease on a BMW.

Ian sighed. "Has he left the stage?"

"No, he's still here somewhere," the AD said.

That was a plus. Ian wouldn't have to go find him on the beach, in a diner, or at LAX trying to board a flight to Bora Bora, all of which had happened in the past.

Ian believed that all actors were crazy. They had to be if they were any good. The truly great ones had to have a manageable version of split personality disorder. How else could they pretend to be someone else so fully that we not only believe it but we invest ourselves emotionally in what they are experiencing?

Ronnie's gift was making unbelievable characters believable. His breakthrough part was playing a dog that switches bodies with a publicist in the movie *Publicity Hound*. Audiences loved seeing Ronnie fetch tennis balls, sniff people's butts, and pee on fire hydrants. That led to one absurd part after another. Ronnie somehow found the heart and the soul in their contrived characters and made them real. He could do that because he became them, which made him crazier than actors who simply became other people. Ian worried about Ronnie's ability to maintain his sanity and felt guilty about his own culpability in exploiting the actor's increasingly shaky mental health. That guilt-ridden concern was what set Ian apart from the other producers on the show and Ronnie probably sensed that. Besides, Ian actually liked Ronnie.

"Okay." Ian got up with a sigh of resignation. At least this was a good excuse to run away from his script. "Where are you shooting?"

"At the police station," the AD said. That was one of the four permanent sets on the soundstage that were used in almost every episode. The other sets were Hollywood's apartment, Vine's house, and the forensics lab. A second soundstage held new sets and the swing sets, the ones redressed from previous episodes to be different interiors. "We're already thirty minutes behind schedule."

"Relax," Ian said. "I'll take care of it."

Ian walked down the hall to the heavy padded door to the stage. He paused before opening the door to make sure that the red light, which indicated shooting was in progress, wasn't on and went inside. He didn't want to be the producer who ruined a scene with his carelessness.

The stage was dark except for the lights from the three-walled police station set, which was all lit up for the next shot. The entire crew of cameramen, grips, makeup artists, and sound engineers was there, waiting around for Ronnie. The director paced behind the cameras while talking animatedly on his cell phone, probably complaining to his agent and begging him to find him a job on a better show.

Ian walked through the dark sets to Vine's apartment, which was essentially a greenhouse with living room furniture, all metal framed, because the character didn't own anything made from wood, for obvious reasons. The only light came from the spillover from the police station set. He found Ronnie sitting in a La-Z-Boy recliner nearly hidden by ferns, his green hair blending in with the leaves.

Ronnie was in his character's jacket and tie, tailored to show off his muscular physique. He had the body of an action hero but the cheerful, rosy-cheeked face of a boy. That was a big part of his appeal. He didn't look so cheerful right now. He looked like he was ready to strangle himself with one of the fake vines that dangled from the ceiling.

Ian smiled. "Hey, Ronnie, how are you doing?"

"Did you come to drag me back to the set?"

"Nope." Ian took a seat on one of the chairs. "I like to come down here when I'm stuck on a scene."

"I didn't know that."

"I usually do it when no one's around. But I'm going through a rough patch right now so here I am."

"Why do you come here?"

"One of the great things about writing a TV show instead of a novel is that it's not all in your head. It physically exists. You can immerse yourself in it. You can sit in a character's house, or go to his office, or even put on his clothes and there you are, right in his world." All of that was true, though it wasn't why he was here right now. "Why are you here?"

"I'm hiding," he said.

"From what?"

"Everybody watching," Ronnie said. "Everywhere I go, someone is looking and listening. I have no peace."

"That's because you're an actor and you're famous. You can't do your job without an audience and you have a big one, so people recognize you," Ian said. "That's the price of success in your business. Or are you talking about the pressure of carrying a show and knowing everybody else's job is to look at you all day for lighting, camera, wardrobe, makeup, or sound?"

"No, it's beyond that." Ronnie lowered the footrest and leaned forward, confiding in Ian. "They're always watching, even when I'm alone and nobody is around. They're listening, too."

"Who are *they*?"

Ronnie shook his head. Either it was too complicated or pointless to explain. "I feel like there's no escape."

Ian nodded, as if he understood, which he didn't. "Sure there is."

"Where?"

"The same place I go. The world of Charlie Vine. But you have it better than me. I can imagine it, and I can sit in it, but you can live it. You can do it right here but especially out there, on the police station set, where the scene is waiting for you to bring it to life."

"Where there are three cameras in my face and a microphone right above my head."

"Only before the director says 'action,' when you're still Ronnie Mancuso," Ian said. "But in the next instant, you're Charlie Vine and that all disappears. It's not a set anymore. There are no cameras or microphones. It's another place, a world of pure imagination."

Ian had to stop himself before he broke into song, though he heard Gene Wilder singing in his head. The sad thing was that, even though none of it was on the page, this was the best writing he'd done all day.

Ronnie glanced toward the glow of lights that illuminated the police station set, then looked back at Ian, acknowledging what he said with a nod. "You're right. Here I'm fine. It's out there in the real world where I have to worry."

"You have nothing to worry about out there, either. You're an actor. They'll only see what you want them to see, and hear what you want them to hear, because you can be anybody you want to be. That's your superpower. The power of illusion."

Ronnie got to his feet and took a deep breath. He was ready to work again. "You're writing the script for next week's show."

"Uh-huh."

"How's it going?"

"I'm down here, sitting in the Vine's house," Ian said. "That should tell you something."

"Great," Ronnie said. "So I'll be getting another shit script that I'll have to save with my performance."

Ronnie winked and walked out. But he was right. That was exactly what would happen.

CHAPTER TWENTY-NINE

Blackthorn Global Security Headquarters, Bethesda, Maryland. July 20. 3:25 p.m. Eastern Standard Time.

Blackthorn's entire media wall was filled with a high-definition bird's-eye view of Klamath Falls, Oregon, from the combat drone's camera, creating the vivid illusion that Cross could walk out of the room and plunge thousands of feet to the ground below. It reminded him of his early days as an operative, leaping out of airplanes into war zones to covertly assist the rebels on the ground in overthrowing their governments. The CIA called it "regime change." It rarely worked but that didn't stop the agency from repeating the mistake.

"The police went to the house in Seattle," Victoria reported, breaking into his thoughts. "They've found a woman's body."

She swiped an image on her screen and it appeared on the media wall in a window within the drone's aerial view. Cross looked up at a crime scene photo of a woman in a black jogging suit, impaled with a fireplace poker on a bloody kitchen floor. It wasn't Margo French.

"Who is she?" he asked.

"It's our asset," Victoria said.

It was unbelievable to him. An obscene practical joke being played on Cross by a cruel God. A trained assassin goes up against a writer with a broken arm and a dog sitter . . . *and loses*? How the hell does that happen?

The only explanation Cross could think of was that his people missed something in their background checks of Ludlow and French. One or both of the targets were trained in self-defense. His money was on Ludlow, based on what was in his Straker books and the fact that he'd survived three attempts on his life. But he wouldn't assume that French didn't have hidden combat skills as well.

When this was over, he'd find the morons who'd made that monumental research blunder and make them pay dearly for it. From now on, though, he'd treat Ludlow and French as if they were professional spies, two Russian sleeper agents on the run. Hell, maybe they were. It made as much sense as anything else that had happened over the last few days.

"Make sure that any fingerprints in the house that don't belong to the owners or the dog sitter come back as dead ends," Cross said. "I don't want the police finding Ludlow before we do."

"No problem," Seth said. "But soon the authorities will discover that the dog sitter has disappeared, if they haven't already. They might even learn that French was escorting Ludlow around Seattle and that he hasn't shown up at his Denver signing."

"Hopefully they'll both be dead before the police get that far along," Cross said. "Do what you can in the meantime to wipe French and Ludlow from the picture and slow the investigation down. Create a fake, unexpected trip for French, perhaps to deal with a death in her family, or something along those lines, to explain her disappearance. Create the entire travel trail, the same as we would to build a cover for an agent. Do the same for Ludlow. Notify Ludlow's publisher and the bookstores on his tour that he's had to cancel his appearances."

"Consider it done," Seth said.

Victoria read some details on her screen. "According to the police reports, the house was ransacked and a vintage 1968 Mustang 390 GT fastback is missing from the garage. They've got an APB out on it."

Cross doubted that would lead anywhere. Ludlow had probably swapped the license plates with another vehicle. That's what a pro would do and, from now on, that's what he was assuming Ludlow was. But why did he pick such a distinctive car? A pro wouldn't want to stand out.

"What other vehicles were in the garage?"

"A 2015 Porsche Panamera, a 2016 Range Rover, and a 2017 Ferrari," Victoria said.

Now it made sense. They were *all* showy cars. But Ludlow chose the only car without electronics and wireless connectivity. Smart move. He wondered if Ludlow had already ditched the car in favor of another, less showy vehicle, something common like a Toyota Corolla or Ford Focus.

"Get a list of any car thefts that occurred in Seattle last night and any that occurred along the route to Klamath Falls," Cross said. "They may have changed vehicles. In the meantime, add the Mustang to the drone's search parameters."

"Yes, sir," Victoria said. "But we need a way to narrow down the search area. They could have gone anywhere after leaving Klamath Falls."

No, not anywhere. Ludlow was definitely going somewhere specific. Cross was certain there was a strategy behind Ludlow's actions. Maybe there had been from the moment he left Los Angeles and they'd missed it. Cross wouldn't underestimate Ludlow again.

"He knows exactly where he's going and what he's doing. There's nothing random about his actions." Cross turned to Seth. "Go through Ludlow's history of credit card statements and phone bills for any charges or calls within a three-hundred-mile radius west, east, and south of Klamath Falls. Go back a decade."

Seth typed a few keys and scanned the results. "Five years ago, he bought a tank of gas with his American Express card in Cedarville, California, and then did it again three days later. He hasn't been back since."

On the big screen, a satellite view of Cedarville appeared. It was barely more than a rest stop on the northeastern edge of California right at the Nevada border.

"What's in Cedarville?" Cross asked.

"The last chance for food and gas before going into the Long Valley region of northwestern Nevada," Seth said, calling up a satellite view of that region on the media wall. It appeared to be nothing but grasslands and dry lake beds.

"And what's out there?"

"A forgotten ghost town and hundreds of miles of wilderness," Seth said. "It's virtually uninhabited."

It was more good news. Cross was beginning to see Ludlow's strategy and it was flawed. Ludlow thought he could disappear in a desolate wasteland when all he'd really done was make himself even easier to find. As an added bonus, Cross wouldn't have to be subtle in his eradication effort. There wouldn't be anyone there to see it.

"Deploy the combat drone over Long Valley," Cross said. "Make sure the missiles are live."

CHAPTER THIRTY

Ronnie gave Ian and Margo the grand tour. He led them out of the kitchen and into a long storeroom filled with pallets and shelves of medical supplies, cleaning materials, and food. He pointed out some items as they passed through the room.

"Antibacterial soap, lime, liquid bleach, heavy-duty garbage bags, kitty litter, paper towels, Tyvek disposable coveralls, baby wipes, bottles of lye, toothpaste, respirator masks, potassium iodate tablets," Ronnie said. "The usual."

"Yeah," Margo said. "Everything you'd find in my pantry."

Ronnie gestured to the food. "Rice, beans, salt, corn, sugar, wheat, honey, chocolate, powdered milk, canned meats, canned fruits, canned vegetables, and plenty of military ready-to-eat meals. The army makes a killer beef stroganoff."

"I'm sure they do," Ian said. "The army is well known for its gourmet chefs."

"Don't be a such a snob," Ronnie said.

Margo paused beside a pallet of boxes, one of which was open and full of movie DVDs. "What's this?"

"I bought the entire DVD inventory of a mom-and-pop video rental place that went out of business in Encino. I also bought the fiction stock of a used bookstore in Reseda," Ronnie said, gesturing to another pallet of boxes. "Entertainment is going to be important for maintaining sanity during the End of Days."

"What about your air, power, and water?" Ian asked. "Where does that come from?"

"The air comes from outside and goes through a nuclear, biological, and chemical filtration system. The intake and ventilation pipes above are concealed within artificial rocks and fake brush, a little trick I learned from my days in Hollywood," Ronnie said. "The shelter is powered by batteries stored here and fed by a camouflaged solar array hidden a quarter of a mile away. There's also a backup generator system that runs on biodiesel fuel. The water is drawn directly from a well beneath us and underground storage tanks."

"What's in here?" Margo pointed to a vault door with a combination lock.

"The essentials for survival once it's safe to go above again." Ronnie entered the combination, spun the wheel, and opened the vault. Inside was a cache of weapons and ammunition, including sniper rifles, AK-47s, handguns, an assortment of combat and hunting knives, hand grenades, rocket-propelled grenades, and two rocket launchers.

"Holy shit," Margo said but she wasn't talking about the weapons. Her eyes were on something else. "Is that pirate treasure?"

Ian followed her gaze to the floor, where a dozen bulging gym bags were lined up against the wall. Two of the bags were partially unzipped, one full of gold coins, the other filled with silver ones. All that was missing was a treasure chest to put them in.

"That's two hundred and fifty thousand dollars in precious metals," Ronnie said. "I'll need money when the smoke clears and it's not like I can run to the ATM."

"What's wrong with cash?" Ian asked.

"After Armageddon, cash is only going to be good for starting fires or wiping your ass," Ronnie said. "Gold and silver will endure."

Ronnie closed the vault and led them to the next room, which had two bunk beds, some dressers, and a bookcase. "This is the bunk room, in case I have a family down the road or friends I want to spare from extermination or extinction."

The next room was a full bathroom with a standing shower, a double sink with a granite countertop, and a toilet. Ian wasn't interested in how the toilet and sewage system worked, though Ronnie proceeded to tell him in detail and with pride. As Ronnie was explaining how his sewage system ground waste and blew it into a septic tank, Margo drifted into the master bedroom and shrieked.

"What the fuck!" she said.

Ian joined Margo and was startled to see a woman, naked under a transparent negligee, lounging on a king-size bed, her legs spread suggestively, drawing attention to her exposed crotch and abundant pubic hair. It took an instant for Ian to realize that she wasn't a woman at all, but an incredibly lifelike silicone sex doll. He walked over to get a better look.

The tiny details were convincing. Her nipples were erect, the imperfectly round areolas ringed with raised gooseflesh. Her skin was sparsely freckled, creased on her knuckles and lightly on her brow. Her teeth were slightly crooked and not overly whitened, perhaps even stained a bit by too much coffee. A tiny scar on her chin from a long-ago accident gave her a touch of character.

The giveaway that she wasn't human, alive or dead, was her open eyes. They were blue, and a touch bloodshot, but there was a flatness to them that was beyond death and utterly inanimate. Even the eyes of a corpse had something in their texture that inexplicably conveyed that they'd once revealed an inner life. He'd learned that the other night when he looked into the assassin's dead face. The other key missing element was moisture, in the mouth and eyes. Even a dead body conveys some sense of liquidity. Ian had learned that unpleasant fact, too, from the assassin.

"That's Wanda," Ronnie said with a big smile. "Isn't she gorgeous?"

"I thought she was a corpse," Margo said.

"She's very much alive," Ronnie said. "Her body temperature is ninety-eight point six and her cooch is motorized."

"You're disgusting," Margo said.

"I'm practical, honey. We all have undeniable urges. After a year or two down here, with pestilence and plague raging up there, you'll be glad to have her for comfort and release."

She gave him a hard look. "What do you mean *I* would?"

Ian's gaze drifted to a set of bookshelves bulging with paperbacks. He immediately spotted the spines of his six Clint Straker novels. Apparently, Ronnie hadn't bought the seventh yet or he was waiting until it came out in paperback.

Ian pulled *Death Has No Mercy* off the shelf. On the cover, a resolute Clint Straker stood against the backdrop of an enormous fireball that contained the skyline of Dubai, a woman in a bikini holding an AK-47, and a speedboat.

He held the book up to Ronnie. "You're waiting until the end of the world to read my books?"

"I've read them all, more than once," Ronnie said. "I fucking love Clint Straker."

"If you've already read them," Margo said, "why are they down here?"

"Because I expect the End of Days will bring hardship and times when I doubt myself. Those books are here to give me strength in moments of despair, to remind me what one man can achieve with just guts and determination."

It was the nicest, most meaningful thing anybody had ever said to Ian about his books.

"Really?" Ian asked. "You mean that?"

"You're a badass," Ronnie said. "A man of action who doesn't give up."

"You mean Straker is," Margo said.

She was right about that. Clint Straker was everything that Ian wasn't. Straker didn't run from danger. He ran toward it. Straker was a born warrior, a samurai in blue jeans. That was never clearer to Ian than right now, hiding in a hole from his enemies, holding that book. And as Ian accepted that, he felt a strong, familiar urge, as real and desperate a need as hunger, thirst, or lust, one that made no sense, not in this place, not at this time.

He wanted to write another Straker novel.

Right now.

CHAPTER THIRTY-ONE

Cross looked down on the Mustang from the drone flying overhead. The dusty green car was parked outside of a cinder-block ranch house and a small corral. From what Cross could tell from structures and equipment on the ground, the ranch existed solely to sustain somebody who wanted to live off the grid. But whoever that was, he was fooling himself. There was nowhere a person could hide if the right people wanted him found.

"The Mustang matches the description of the stolen car," Seth said. "However, the plates are registered to a 1998 Ford F-150 pickup in Seattle. Ludlow must have swapped the plates before he left the city."

"He did," Victoria said, excitement in her voice. "We have a match on all of the RFIDs from the groceries purchased in Klamath Falls. They're still in the trunk of the Mustang. We also have hits on Ludlow and French's credit cards coming from inside the house, along with three active heat signatures."

She hit some keys on her keyboard and the heat signatures showed up as red pulses in the house on the screen. The people in the house were moving around.

"That must be Ludlow, French, and whoever lives there," Cross said. "Do we have any idea who the owner is?"

"The property is owned through various shell corporations," Seth said. "It'll take some time to find the real person."

It would be nice to know who else he was killing but it wasn't a priority. Removing Ludlow and French from the playing field was all that mattered to Cross right now.

"It can wait," Cross said. "Rain hell upon them."

Victoria tapped a key. A Hellfire missile shot out from the drone and hit the house dead center. The house exploded, spitting flaming debris in all directions and igniting the nearby propane tank, which erupted in an enormous fireball.

⊕

The explosions were deafening and rocked the underground shelter hard, nearly knocking Ian, Margo, and Ronnie off their feet. It was like they were on rough water. Actually, more like *underwater*. The sense of being in a submarine was so strong that Ian's first, irrational thought was that torpedoes had just missed them and hit the ocean floor. He suspected that he wasn't far from the truth.

"Holy shit," Margo said, her eyes wide with fear.

But Ronnie whooped with delight, a big grin on his face. "That's the New World Order knocking on my door. It's about fucking time."

He ran back to the main room, Ian and Margo right behind him. They all stopped in front of the big-screen TV and stared at the multiple camera feeds. Ronnie's house was obliterated. All that was left of it was a smoking crater and bits of flaming debris scattered all over the compound. One of the cows was on fire, running around the corral, sending up smoke signals. For Ian, seeing the destruction on TV made it seem unreal, as if they were watching something he'd written instead of something that was actually happening. But if he'd written it, who was the hero?

Ian glanced at the paperback of *Death Has No Mercy* in his hand. The tagline read: *Nothing stands in his way. The only fear Straker knows is what he sees in the eyes of his enemies.*

He looked up again and saw Ronnie grinning. Ronnie wasn't angry that his home was destroyed—he was thrilled. Everything he believed was finally coming true.

Ian had always suspected that the happiest day of a survivalist's life would be the one when the world ended. Now he knew it was true. It was validation for all of Ronnie's psychological suffering and proof that he wasn't crazy.

"Is that the best you've got, you pussies?" Ronnie yelled gleefully at the ceiling. "Bring it on."

◉

Cross looked down on the destruction like a malevolent God hurling lightning bolts from the heavens at the mortals who displeased him. This is what happens when you incur my wrath, he thought. The destruction gave Cross a hard-on, which, fortunately, nobody noticed because everyone's attention was on-screen. Even so, he put his hands in his pockets to puff out his pants. He glanced at Victoria and wondered if she got off on it, too. She'd probably go home tonight and whip the skin off the back of some lucky bastard.

The smoke cleared on the screen. He saw the crater where the house had once stood. Ludlow, French, and whomever they'd come to visit were now bone fragments and clumps of charred flesh. The backstory on this operation was finally erased. Now all that was left to deal with were the politics, though in some ways he favored this kind of action. It was clear and decisive.

He saw the Mustang, covered in dust and ash, its windows shattered, but otherwise intact. Not good.

"Take out the Mustang," Cross told Victoria. "I don't want to leave any tracks that lead back to Ludlow or Seattle."

Victoria tapped a key. Another Hellfire missile flew from the drone. The explosion wiped out the car and left another crater. It was like using a tank to kill a fly but at least now the car and its contents were dust.

"Bring the drone home and send a team to collect whatever's left of the bodies for fingerprint, dental, and DNA analysis," Cross said. "I want irrefutable confirmation of the kills."

⌖

Long Valley, Nevada. July 20. 4:15 p.m. Pacific Standard Time.

They waited thirty minutes after the drone flew away before they decided it was safe to leave the bunker and go above. Even so, Ronnie insisted on being armed. He took one of the rocket-propelled grenade launchers with him from the vault. Ian brought his Straker paperback.

They emerged to scorched earth, two craters, and smoking rubble. The pickup truck was engulfed in flames but the bulldozer and tractor remained, seemingly undamaged. The air reeked of burning rubber, wood, gasoline, and cow flesh. Margo squatted and picked up a few coins from the blackened earth.

"I'm sorry, Ronnie," Ian said. "I shouldn't have come here. I brought this on you."

"It's not your fault," Ronnie said. "This day was coming sooner or later and I was getting tired of waiting for it. But it's not over. They'll be back."

Ian knew he was right. They would come for their remains and to clean up the crime scene. He wondered how long they had before the cleaners arrived. A couple of hours? A day? The thought made him look at the book in his hand. Clint Straker would relish the fight. Ian would, too, if he were writing it instead of living it. The fights were the scenes that every reader waited for and they almost wrote themselves. That's because Straker was totally in his element, one man up against impossible odds, armed only with his determination and cunning. God, how Ian wished he were writing that scene now instead of standing there.

"We have to get out of here." Margo nodded at the bulldozer and tractor. "Those aren't going to get us very far and the bad guys will notice right away if they're missing. We'll have to go on foot and try to cover our tracks behind us."

"I've got a big woody," Ronnie said.

"Good for you," Margo said, annoyed. "Is it that time of day for you or are you aroused by the idea of us running into the mountains and dying of exposure?"

Clint Straker doesn't run from anything.

That thought made Ian understand why he had such a strong urge to write. He didn't want to escape the situation he was in. He wanted to beat it, the way Straker would. He looked down at the book in his hand, the one he wrote about the character he created. And in that moment, a chill passed over him, taking with it all of his anxieties. He knew what he had to do.

"I'm talking about the 1974 Ford Country Squire station wagon that I've got hidden in a cave," Ronnie said. "Cars manufactured after 1975 all have electronic ignitions that'll be fried by an EMP blast. This one is blast safe and it has wood veneer paneling on the body."

"Oh," Margo said. "*That* kind of woody. Let's find the car, fill it with your weapons and treasure, and get the hell out of here."

"No," Ian said. "We're done running."

"What's the alternative?" Margo said. "Hide in Ronnie's shelter for a year or two until they forget about us?"

Ian held up his paperback. "Clint Straker wouldn't run and he wouldn't hide."

"You aren't Clint Straker," she said.

"Everybody keeps telling me that but you're wrong," he said. "I *am* Clint Straker. I created him. Everything he is, everything he's ever done, came from within me."

"He's imaginary." She grabbed the book out of his hand and flung it like a Frisbee into the burning wreckage of the pickup truck. "You made up his past and everything that he does. You don't actually have his training or combat experience."

"I have something more important. I know how he thinks and how he reacts. He doesn't wait for things to happen. He *makes* them happen," Ian said. "It's time I stopped thinking like me and started thinking like him."

"That's it, man, get into character." Ronnie clapped Ian on the back. "I got so into the Vine that by episode thirteen, I was capable of photosynthesis."

Margo gave Ronnie a cold, hard look. "You can convert sunlight into energy."

Ronnie held out his arms and tipped his face up to the sky "The sun is my Big Mac."

"Oh, for God's sake," Margo said. "Get real. We're talking about our lives here."

"That's why it's time to embrace our true selves and harness our potential," Ronnie said. He turned to Ian. "So, buddy, there's one question you've got to ask yourself. What would Clint Straker do right now?"

"He'd take the fight to them," Ian said.

"Damn right he would," Ronnie said. "It's going to be the three of us against the C-I-fucking-A."

"That's suicide," Margo said.

"Actually, it sounds just like a Clint Straker book to me," Ian said. "All I need to do is plot it."

Margo took a deep breath, and when she spoke, it was in a calm, patronizing tone, like she was talking to a child. "When you're writing a book, you're in complete control of the universe. It doesn't work like that in the real world."

"Is that so? Tell that to the CIA. If they could use my story idea to kill people in the real world, why can't I do the same thing to bring the CIA down? Someone has to make them pay." Ian tore the duct tape off his cast, pulling chunks of plaster away and throwing them on the ground until his pale, bone-thin right arm was revealed. He stretched his arm out and made a fist. "It's going to be me."

Ian sounded just like Straker and he knew why—because he was, and always had been, Straker inside. For the first time since this nightmare began, he felt strong and unafraid. Ronnie and Margo could see it, too.

Ronnie raised his RPG launcher. "I'm right there with you, man."

Margo looked at Ian for a long moment as she thought it over and then sighed with resignation as she came to a decision that she appeared to already regret. "If we're dead anyway, we might as well go down fighting."

"We're going to have to work on your winning attitude," Ian said.

CHAPTER THIRTY-TWO

The enemy came in an unmarked black helicopter a couple of hours later. They flew in from the south and circled twice over the charred ruins and smoking craters before landing about fifty yards from the compound.

Two men emerged from the helicopter wearing dark sunglasses and white jumpsuits, white gloves, and white rubber boots. They both carried toolboxes that Ian presumed, based on his extensive experience watching police procedurals on television, were evidence-collection kits.

Ian and Margo crouched side by side and watched the men from under a camouflaged tarp that was spread over several artificial boulders atop one of the rocky hillsides that bordered the compound. It was where Ronnie had been hiding when Ian and Margo drove in that morning.

Margo used binoculars to track the men while Ian watched them through the scope on the rocket-propelled grenade launcher that rested on his shoulder. The RPG launcher was essentially a tube with a rocket stuck in the front and a trigger on the bottom. Ronnie had given Ian and Margo a quick lesson in how to use it. It wasn't a complex device.

Ian shifted his aim to the helicopter, putting the craft in the center of his sights. It would be a hard target to miss.

The weapon was too heavy for Ian's weak right arm so he propped the end of it on a rock in front of him, took a deep breath, and squeezed the trigger.

The rocket shot out, the blazing backfire scorching the rocks behind Ian. An instant later the rocket slammed into the helicopter and blew it apart. The concussive force of the explosion knocked the two men off their feet, which was fortunate, because a split second later a severed rotor blade sliced through the air where they'd stood. The two men landed facedown on the ground. They lifted their heads and saw Ronnie under the tractor, smiling and pointing an AK-47 at their heads.

"Keep kissing the dirt, assholes," he said. "Hands behind your backs."

Up in their hideout on the hill, Margo grinned at Ian. "That was great."

He grinned back at her. "Now you know why my books are best-sellers. I can plot."

But writing it didn't compare to the exhilaration of actually *doing* it. The gleeful expression on Margo's face told him that she enjoyed the visceral experience as much as he did even though she hadn't pulled the trigger. It just proved what everybody in Hollywood already knew: everybody loves an explosion.

Ian and Margo rose from their hiding place and made their way carefully down through the rocks to the ground, where Ronnie stood over the two men with his AK-47 aimed at their backs.

"Be still, boys," Ronnie said. "One twitch of my finger and you're both vulture chow."

Ian and Margo removed zip ties from their pockets and they each took a man, first binding their wrists, then rolling them over onto their backs. The two men, dirt sticking to their sweaty faces, scowled furiously at their captors.

"It could be worse," Margo told the two men. "We could have shot you out of the sky."

Ian got the feeling that she would have been okay with that, too.

He and Margo opened the men's jumpsuits and searched their pockets, retrieving wallets, key fobs, and photo IDs. Margo stood up and flipped through the wallet that she'd found.

"This one is Edwin Pessel." Margo nodded at the man at her feet. "He's a security specialist for Blackthorn Global Security in Las Vegas."

That didn't make sense to Ian. What did Blackthorn have to do with the CIA?

Ian opened the other man's wallet and found another Blackthorn ID. "This one is Stuart Bowers. He also works at Blackthorn."

"Of course they do," Ronnie said.

Ian put his foot on Bowers' chest to keep him down and looked at Ronnie. "Why 'of course'?"

"Because Blackthorn is the SS of the New World Order. It's full of ex-spies, ex-politicians, war criminals, disgraced scientists, and professional psychopaths. Their job is to terrorize the populace so that they are so scared that they will gladly give up their freedoms in exchange for the false promise of safety."

"And you think these guys do that by flying jets into buildings," Margo said.

"That's one way," Ronnie said. "The Kennedy, King, and Elvis assassinations, Watergate, AIDS, Botox, crop circles, the Ebola epidemic, opioid addiction, and genetically engineered fruit are just some of their greatest hits."

"You left out artificial sweeteners," Margo said.

"Because that goes without saying," Ronnie said.

Blackthorn was a plot twist that Ian didn't see coming. It changed his perspective about everything that had happened since Bob first knocked on his door. It also gave him hope. "What if it's Blackthorn, not the CIA, that crashed the plane and is trying to kill us?"

"So what?" Ronnie said. "They're both puppets of the New World Order."

"I don't see how that makes things any better for us, either," Margo said.

"It's a game changer. I've met the man in charge of this conspiracy but I don't know his name or anything about him." Ian looked down at Bowers, who glowered at him from under his foot. "Now we have a way to find out."

Ronnie and Margo worked fast. She helped him bring up all the weapons, ammo, and other supplies that they needed from the bunker while Ian stood guard with the AK-47 over Pessel and Bowers, who remained bound and on their backs in the dirt. Ronnie dismantled the bunker's surveillance system with a sledgehammer. Then he and Margo gathered up anything inside that could be used as a weapon or a tool, piled it all into the vault, and locked it up. When Ronnie and Margo came back to the surface, Ian told Pessel and Bowers to get to their feet and ordered them down the stairs.

Ian, Margo, and Ronnie gathered around the hatch and looked down at the two Blackthorn operatives, who now appeared more fearful than angry.

"Here's what's going to happen," Ian said. "We're going to park the tractor on the hatch and leave, trapping you in that bunker. The good news is, after you break those zip ties, you can survive down there for years."

"Assuming you like freeze-dried beef stroganoff," Margo said. "And don't kill each other fighting over the sex doll."

"But first," Ian said, "you're going to tell us how to get into Blackthorn's building in Las Vegas, access their computers, and find photos of their senior employees without getting caught."

"Why the fuck would we do that?" Pessel asked, practically spitting out the words.

"Because if we get captured or killed, nobody will ever know you're down there," Ian said. "You'll be buried alive for years."

"When the food runs out, one of you will murder the other for the meat," Ronnie said. "But that'll only buy you a few more weeks of solitary confinement, thinking about the savage thing you've done and knowing you're going to starve anyway, dying in wretched agony while you desperately suck the last speck of marrow from another man's bones."

"What a horrible way to die," Margo said. "I can't imagine what it would be like."

But Pessel and Bowers could. They told Ian everything he wanted to know.

CHAPTER THIRTY-THREE

Ronnie and Margo took turns driving the 1974 Ford Country Squire on the ten-and-a-half-hour journey to Las Vegas. He drove the first four-hour stretch, southwest into California so they could travel on paved roads, then due south for two hundred miles on US 395 before they veered east again, crossing back into Nevada. They rolled into Reno at about 8:00 p.m. and stopped at a Goodwill store. Ronnie reluctantly ditched his aluminum foil helmet before he and Ian went inside. The men bought used business suits, ties, and dress shoes while Margo went to a gas station and got them some food at Carl's Jr.

Margo picked them up and stayed behind the wheel as they headed southeast, stopping four hours later at a Shell station in Tonopah, Nevada, which was on the northwestern edge of the 4,530-square-mile US military range for aircraft gunnery training, aerial bombardment, nuclear weapons testing, and army combat exercises. Their proximity to all of that secret military hardware and testing made Ronnie very nervous. He desperately wanted to put his aluminum-foil helmet back on but Ian convinced him it would draw too much attention to them. While Margo refilled the gas tank, Ian and Ronnie went to the restroom, where Ronnie shaved off his beard and they both changed into their Goodwill suits.

Ronnie took over the driving and put his helmet back on. Nobody argued with him about the helmet. It was fine for him to wear it in the car. Ian figured the helmet was like a security blanket for him and he couldn't blame Ronnie for feeling anxious. Ian wished he had a security blanket of his own and thought about sucking his thumb instead but it wasn't something Clint Straker would ever do. Margo hummed to herself for relaxation. It wasn't a song Ian recognized so he assumed it was one of her own compositions.

They reached Las Vegas at 3:00 a.m., cutting across the city to Henderson Executive Airport, a popular hub for corporate and private aircraft. This was where the helicopter and corporate jet used by Blackthorn's Las Vegas office were based. Ronnie parked the station wagon beside the black Suburban that Pessel had driven to the airport. It was Bowers who'd flown the helicopter.

Ronnie took off his helmet and the three of them got out of the station wagon. Ian pointed Pessel's key fob at the Suburban and unlocked it. He took a deep breath and tossed the key fob to Ronnie so he could drive.

"Now comes the fun part," Ian said.

"Good luck," Margo said.

"They're the ones who are going to need it," Ian said.

It was a Straker line, and it made Margo roll her eyes, but Ian liked how it sounded coming from his mouth. He and Ronnie walked toward the Suburban. It was a hero moment. Ronnie, being an actor, instinctively knew it, too, and it showed in his confident stride.

"Wait," Margo said and both men stopped. She went up to them and yanked the tags that dangled from their right sleeves. "You forgot to take off the price tags."

That completely deflated the hero moment but it didn't shake their confidence. Ian and Ronnie got into the Suburban and they drove toward the glittering Las Vegas skyline.

Las Vegas, Nevada. July 21. 3:35 a.m. Pacific Standard Time.

Blackthorn provided enhanced security services for several casinos and operated out of a new six-story building in downtown Las Vegas, a block west of the Plaza Hotel. It was one of the first buildings in an envisioned "world-class" office park, the latest attempt by the city to rejuvenate the heart of Old Town after a $70 million light-show canopy over Fremont Street didn't generate much of a pulse.

Ronnie stopped in front of the garage gate and next to a camera mounted beside the driveway. He rolled down his window and held up Pessel's ID to the camera so that it blocked most of his face from being seen by the lone, bored security guard on duty.

The guard was stationed at a desk in the lobby and noted the name on the ID that filled the screen. He glanced at his computer. A scanner at the gate identified the Suburban as a Blackthorn vehicle that had been checked out by Pessel earlier that day. The ID and vehicle matched. Everything checked out. The guard hit the button to raise the gate and went back to watching *Game of Thrones* on his laptop.

Ronnie drove into the garage. The first floor was filled with a fleet of identical black Suburbans and a few black Audi sedans. He parked in an empty space by the elevator and the two men got out, angling their bodies and faces away from the security cameras. Pessel and Bowers had told them where every camera was positioned. The operatives also assured them that there was little chance of anybody being in the building at that hour besides the guard in the lobby.

The elevator opened and the two men stepped inside. Ian held Bowers' ID up to the scanner and hit the button for the fifth floor. The doors slid closed, indicating that the ID checked out and they had clearance to enter the building. The elevator went up, fast and smooth, into the belly of the beast.

Margo pulled into the parking lot of the Main Street Station Casino and drove to one of the empty spaces along the far end, facing the office park. She positioned the station wagon at an angle so that the security camera mounted on the nearest light post wouldn't be able to get a clear look at her face. She got out, opened the door to the back seat, and slid out the rocket-propelled grenade launcher that was under a blanket on the floor.

She crouched on the ground beside the station wagon, which hid her from the camera, balanced the rocket launcher on her shoulder, and aimed at the Blackthorn building. She didn't have any experience shooting rocket launchers but she wasn't worried. Ronnie had taught her the basics of using the weapon and she had a very big target. If she didn't get a signal from Ronnie in five minutes, she'd blow a hole in the sixth floor to draw the authorities and flush out everybody who was inside.

The elevator opened on a wide, long floor filled with dozens of empty cubicles and lined with floor-to-ceiling windows. Ian and Ronnie had an unobstructed view from Glitter Gulch to the end of the Strip, where the Luxor pyramid shot a spotlight into outer space, beckoning any extraterrestrials who enjoyed blackjack, strippers, and all-you-can-eat buffets.

The lights were on and both men were keenly aware of the surveillance cameras mounted on the pillars around the room. The men had to assume that the guard in the lobby was watching them, out of boredom if nothing else, so they had to be careful not to do anything suspicious.

Ian went to Pessel's cubicle, sat down in front of the computer, and entered the operative's user ID and password. He was just a weary agent filing a late report. While he did that, Ronnie went to a window facing

Glitter Gulch, positioning his body so the nearest camera wouldn't catch what he was about to do. He took a Maglite out of his pocket and flashed it twice at the Main Street Casino. Margo flashed back twice in return from the parking lot. Now she knew they'd safely entered the building and they knew that she had their backs.

Ian followed the instructions that Pessel had given him and called up the employee list. The names were linked to individual pages with the employee's photo, short biography, and contact information. He started with the senior executives, calling up each entry until he saw Bob's face. It didn't take long. Ian was on his fourth name when Bob's picture came up. He felt an immediate jolt of recognition. Bob's real name was Wilton Cross, and based on his brief biography, Ian knew they wouldn't have found out his identity if they hadn't come here. Cross was a man who lived in the shadows, who stayed out of the public eye and didn't exist in Google search results. He was also a man who crashed planes into cities and sent out assassins to kill novelists.

"I've got him," Ian said. "His name, his phone numbers, everything we need."

Ronnie came up behind him and looked over his shoulder. "Let's see the bastard."

"Meet Wilton Cross. He works in Blackthorn's Bethesda, Maryland, headquarters as their global chief of covert operations. He spent two decades doing the same dirty job for the CIA."

"I told you the CIA and Blackthorn were the same thing."

Ian wanted a picture of Cross. He tried to print out the web page but his access to do so was denied. "There's a crucial difference. Blackthorn is a business. They didn't crash that plane into Waikiki for ideology or patriotism. They did it for their bottom line."

"World domination."

"The almighty dollar." Ian tried to do a screen grab but that was also denied. He didn't have a phone to take a photo of Cross' picture on the screen so he settled for writing his phone numbers and address on a piece of paper and then logged out of the computer. "There's a money-making angle to this somewhere. I don't know what it is but it may be the key to taking this bastard down. Or there might be another way."

"I have the other way." Ronnie opened his jacket to show Ian the gun holstered on his belt. "We drive to Bethesda, walk up behind him, and shoot him in the back of the head."

"That would be murder."

"He deserves it. The guy is responsible for killing hundreds of people."

"But if we execute Cross, we won't be able to prove that and we'll go to prison."

"You're a writer," Ronnie said. "You'll come up with something."

Ian hoped so, because at the moment he had no plan and nothing to go on except a name and a face.

"Let's get out of here." Ian got up from his seat and the two men went to the elevator. It opened immediately.

They took the elevator down to the parking garage and got back into the Suburban and Ronnie drove them out, flashing his headlights twice as they emerged as a signal to Margo. As they headed away, Ian lowered his window and adjusted the side-view mirror so he could see the building receding behind them.

They were a block away when the rocket-propelled grenade streaked from the Main Street Station Casino parking lot and slammed into the fifth floor of the Blackthorn building, the explosion blowing out the windows in a belch of fire and raining glass onto the empty street below.

Ian and Ronnie shared a smile.

"That'll get their attention," Ian said.

"I'm so glad you came to visit," Ronnie said.

CHAPTER THIRTY-FOUR

Ronnie drove two miles north to a strip club that was famous for having totally nude dancers of both sexes. Ian heard that it was run by a criminal defense attorney who'd taken the club as payment for defending the owner, who was serving a life sentence for murdering the previous owner, who, in turn, was rumored to have killed the owner who'd preceded him. That was Las Vegas. The club was located between a motel and a pawnshop, both also owned by the attorney, both also taken in lieu of fees from clients in cases he ultimately lost. That was Las Vegas, too. In a decade, the attorney might own the entire city.

Ronnie pulled in to the strip club parking lot and found a spot in the back, near the motel. Ian and Ronnie got out. A moment later, Margo arrived in the station wagon and nearly jumped out of the car with excitement.

"What else can we blow up?" she asked.

"That's the problem with using explosives," Ronnie said. "It's like jerking off, eating potato chips, or watching *Match Game*. Once you start, you can't stop."

"It feels great to strike back instead of running," Ian said. "Now they can start being afraid."

"Do we know who we're scaring?" Margo said.

"Wilton Cross. He's the man who recruited me and the three other writers," Ian said. "He's the one we have to take down."

"How are we going to do that?" Ronnie asked.

"With a rocket, I hope," Margo said.

"We can't beat them with our weapons," Ian said. "Our only option is to turn their strength into their weakness and—"

Margo interrupted him. "Use their own force against them. Yeah, yeah, I know all that shit. It's straight out of your Straker books."

"It's also the ancient philosophy behind judo and other martial arts," Ian said.

"I know that, too." She put her hands on her hips and faced Ian. "But what does that blah blah blah actually mean for us? How are we going to take down Blackthorn?"

"You mean the jackbooted army of the New World Order," Ronnie said.

"I mean the professional assassins who want to kill us and will find us anywhere we try to hide."

"I'll let you know as soon as I've worked out the fine points," Ian said. "But the first step is to get out of Las Vegas."

Bethesda, Maryland. July 21. 7:49 a.m. Eastern Standard Time.

Wilton Cross' kitchen smelled like a bakery. Just breathing the air was fattening. The grandchildren were coming over that afternoon so his wife, Sarah, was baking a cake for them. She'd started on it immediately after preparing fried eggs, crispy bacon, buttermilk biscuits, a bowl of strawberries, and fresh-ground coffee for her husband, Wilton, who was eating his breakfast at the kitchen table while reading the *Washington Post* and watching Fox News.

He wore a red cardigan, one of the dozens in various colors and patterns that Sarah had bought for him. It was the kind of sweater that Hugh Beaumont, Fred MacMurray, and Robert Young used to wear while playing sitcom dads. Nobody wore them anymore, not even on TV, but his wife insisted that he change into one as soon as he walked through the front door when he got home from the office. It fit with her manufactured and comforting image of him as an average family man, an insurance salesman perhaps, coming home from work. She didn't want to think about what he actually did. All she knew was that he worked for the government and that he couldn't talk about his job. But she wasn't stupid. He wouldn't have married her if she were.

They'd met when they were both students in their twenties at Yale, where she majored in classical civilization, concentrating on Greek literature, and he studied political science with an emphasis on international relations. His studies had served him well in his current profession but her literary interests these days were limited to the prodigious output of Nora Roberts and Janet Evanovich.

Sarah was gray-haired now and her skin was lined but she'd managed to keep her slim figure as she'd aged. If Cross squinted, and imagined away the apron that she always wore, he could see the same woman he'd married decades ago. He did a lot of imagining when they were in bed and he was sure that she did, too. He'd aged and fattened over time and knew that he'd grown more emotionally distant. That's because now there was far more of his life that he couldn't share with her than there was that he could. There was nothing about her that he didn't know. What she didn't tell him he knew from the surveillance devices that watched her in the house and car and recorded her conversations on the phone.

Wilton had spent the night at home and was planning to spend the day there as well, because he was no longer in "crisis mode" at the office.

Ludlow was dead and the operation was moving into the political phase, which was scripted and would unfold without him having to do anything.

The bodies of Ayoub Darwish and Habib Ebrahimi, the men framed for downing the TransAmerican flight, had already arrived at Andrews Air Force Base. Their computers and cell phones were being analyzed by Blackthorn, which was redundant, since they were the ones who'd loaded them with the fraudulent e-mails, files, and photos that would prove that the terrorist group Harakat Ahrar al-Sham al-Islamiyya was behind the crash and was planning more attacks. The CIA's ineptitude and grave operational shortcomings, and the threat they presented to the nation's security, would soon be abundantly clear to the Senate Intelligence Committee and to the president . . . if they weren't already.

Although the cause of the plane crash, and the key persons responsible for it, had been identified, none of that information had been released publicly yet. It was still top secret until all of the facts were known by investigators and it was decided how the credit for the discoveries would be divvied up among the players for maximum political gain. So far, only the information about the hacking device implanted in the Gordon-Ganza 877 aircraft had gone public. That was the news that dominated the front page of the *Washington Post* this morning. On TV, Cross watched as Fox's Shepard Smith reported the details while showing video of grounded jets sitting on the tarmac at major airports.

SMITH: All Gordon-Ganza 877s worldwide have been grounded, effective immediately, until each plane can be searched for a device that allows terrorists to remotely access the autopilot system. Any 877s still flying in US airspace are being escorted to the nearest landing strips by fighter jets. Airports around the world are packed with stranded travelers. A travel nightmare like this has not been seen since 9/11.

"Do we have to listen to this?" Sarah said, stirring something in a mixing bowl. "I want to see upbeat, happy things before the grandchildren visit. We don't want that negativity in our minds or in the house."

"You're right. I'm sorry, dear."

Cross picked up the remote and switched to HGTV. *Property Brothers* was on. It was a show about twin brothers who renovated houses.

Sarah brightened immediately. She loved those renovation shows. Since she started watching HGTV, she'd remodeled their kitchen four times. He suspected she did it just so she could feel like she was participating in the action. She'd be able to do it a fifth time, and hire those freakish twins to do the work, with the money he'd be getting soon.

His cell phone rang. He got up and stepped into the backyard before answering it. Sarah didn't like it when he talked "business" in the house.

"Yes?" he said.

"There was an explosion this morning at our Las Vegas office," Seth said. "No one was hurt but the damage is extensive."

He didn't believe in coincidences. Yesterday, they'd killed Ludlow, French, and whomever they went to see in Nevada. Today there was an explosion in their Las Vegas office. Cross knew the blast had to be related in some way to that incident. But how? Had Ludlow somehow figured out that it was Blackthorn that was pursuing him? Was there something on the assassin in Seattle that tipped him off? Did Ludlow get word out to someone before he was killed? How much did this unknown person know?

"What was the cause of the blast?" Cross asked.

"The fire department hasn't determined that yet," Seth replied. "They're still fighting the flames. I'm hacking into surveillance cameras in the area to see what they can tell us."

Ludlow was dead but the problem still wasn't contained. There was another Rogue Element in play. Stomach acid rose quickly in his throat and he swallowed it down before he gagged. Stress aggravated his acid reflux, especially after a big meal. He didn't need this.

"Where's the team that we sent out to Long Valley?"

"Agents Edwin Pessel and Stuart Bowers," Seth said. "According to our security logs, they were the last people to enter and leave the building, minutes before the blast."

"What do they have to say for themselves?"

"We haven't been able to reach them but we've located their car. It's in the parking lot of a strip club downtown."

Something was very wrong with this picture. Cross swallowed back more acid.

"Send some agents to the club and drag those two out. I want to talk to them. In the meantime, get our drone back over the strike zone. I want another look at it. I'll be right in."

He ended the call and went back inside to look for some Tums. He had a bad feeling he'd need handfuls of them today.

CHAPTER THIRTY-FIVE

Primm, Nevada. July 21. 5:30 a.m. Pacific Standard Time.

There were three casino/hotels off the I-15 on the Nevada side of the border with California: Whiskey Pete's, Buffalo Bill's, and the Primm Valley Resort. Depending on which direction you were traveling, Primm was either your first or last chance to gamble before crossing the state line.

Margo drove. She hadn't said much since she'd picked up Ronnie and Ian. She'd come down from her adrenaline high about twenty miles outside of Las Vegas. Ronnie was asleep in the back seat, snoring loudly and wearing his aluminum foil helmet again.

Margo stole a glance into the rearview mirror at Ronnie, then a sideways look at Ian in the passenger seat, before returning her attention to the road. Ian could tell that she had something on her mind.

"I have a question for you," she said. "When Ronnie left LA for Nevada, why did you go after him and try to talk him into coming back?"

"I thought he was mentally ill and needed help."

"Now what do you think?"

"He might be the sanest man I know."

"That's scary," she said.

"After everything we've been through, *that's* what scares you?"

"Yeah. Because I'm beginning to think you're right." She gave him a quick, worried glance. "What does that say about us?"

"This is a crazy world, Margo. Maybe you need to be a little crazy to see it."

"I wish I couldn't see it. Then nobody would be shooting missiles at me." She smiled and then shook her head, as if in disagreement with herself. "That sounds crazy, too."

"Not given our situation," Ian said.

"You're right. I bet there's nothing either one of us could say right now that wouldn't come off sounding insane."

"We're going to Los Angeles," Ian said.

"That's a perfect example," she said. "In any other context, that simple statement about the direction we're driving wouldn't sound like the ranting of a drooling, bug-eyed lunatic."

"I'm serious. That's where we're going."

Margo gave him a hard look that somehow captured her anger, her dismay, and her fatigue. It was quite a look. "That's the worst possible place for us to go."

She didn't end her statement with *you moron* but it was heavily implied in her patronizing tone of voice.

"It's my home," Ian said. "Not that I have an actual home there anymore. Blackthorn blew it up."

"Take the subtle hint. They'll be watching every place you've ever been and everyone you've ever known. You can't go back."

"I ran away. Straker wouldn't do that. So I can't do that."

"That's stupid," she said. "Hey, I have an idea. Why not save time, call Cross, and tell him exactly where to send his killers?"

She didn't mean it, of course. But once she said it, Ian knew that she was right. It was the perfect Straker move in this situation. All he had to do was figure out what happened next. The key was to think of it as a story, just like all the others that he'd plotted.

"You may be on to something," he said.

Margo sighed, relieved. "I'm glad you're listening to reason. I'll take the first exit that comes along and head in another direction."

"That's not what I meant. I'm talking about telling Cross where to find us."

"I was being sarcastic," she said.

"You were being creative. Sometimes the best stories come when your character makes the worst possible decision. I think this is one of those times."

She was silent for a few miles and when she spoke again, she was calm and serious.

"I'll take you to Los Angeles. But once we get there, you'll have an hour to convince me that your scheme works." There was nothing patronizing about her tone of voice but her mental and emotional fatigue were even more evident. "I've come with you this far but I won't let you get me killed. I'll bail out before that can happen."

He knew she meant it. Frankly, he was surprised she'd stuck with him this long.

"I understand," he said. "Fate is a bastard. Never let him choose how you'll die."

"You can think like Clint Straker if you want," she said. "But I'll punch you in the face if you talk like him again."

He knew she meant that, too.

Bethesda, Maryland. July 21. 8:30 a.m. Eastern Standard Time.

Cross stormed into the control center. He'd left the house so quickly that he'd forgotten to take off his cardigan. "What have you got?"

Victoria and Seth shared a look. Neither one of them wanted to deliver the bad news. But Victoria had more guts and enjoyed inflicting pain. This was going to hurt Cross.

"Agents Pessel and Bowers weren't in the strip club. We don't know where they are. But we know Pessel logged in to his computer before the blast and we know what he was looking at."

"Show me," Cross said.

Victoria swiped something off her screen and onto the media wall. Cross looked up and saw his own face staring back at him like a huge reflection. Pessel had no reason to be interested in Cross' biography, his location, or his photo. But Cross knew one man who did. A dead man.

"Is the drone over the strike zone yet?" Cross asked.

"It's arriving now." Victoria typed something on her keyboard and Cross' picture on the media wall was replaced by the drone's camera view.

The drone came around a hill of boulders and over the ruins of the compound, revealing the charred hulk of a helicopter that had obviously been blown apart.

The room instantly fell silent, everyone stopping what they were doing to absorb what they were seeing on-screen and the implications. Someone had shot down the helicopter with a rocket.

Before Cross, or anybody else, could give it too much thought, the drone banked over the site, and as it came around again something else came into view. Two words were written on the ground in large, jagged letters formed out of pieces of blackened rubble.

FUCK YOU!

CHAPTER THIRTY-SIX

The drone kept circling the wreckage and the profane taunt. Cross felt the heat on his face, flushed with fury. Ludlow was still alive and giving him the finger. How had he survived?

"Do you want us to send another team out there to clean that up?" Victoria asked.

"Absolutely not," Cross said. "There's been too much activity out there already. The less we do to draw attention to that desolate spot, the better. If we leave it alone, it will probably be years before anybody stumbles across it. Besides, we don't know what booby traps Ludlow might have set. I'd rather some hiker or coyote set them off than lose any more of our people or equipment."

"How can he still be alive?" Seth said.

"Because everything we know about Ludlow is a lie. He's somebody else entirely. Someone with extensive training, a professional," Cross said, then addressed all the operatives in the room. "And you all missed it and gave me bad intel. You fucked up and now three of our people are dead because of it. That's on you. Your priority, the only reason you exist on this earth, is to take down Ian Ludlow, whoever he really is. Tear apart his history and find his real one. I want to know where, when, and how he acquired his skills. I want to know his real agenda. He's played us. I want to know why and how so it never happens to us again. It's obvious that he writes those Straker books based on personal experience. Analyze every word that he's written. His real story is between the lines."

"I'll start pulling up camera feeds from casino, business, and intersection cameras around our Las Vegas office," Seth said. "I'll see if I can identify the car he's driving now and find out where he's hiding or what direction he's heading in."

"You can do that," Cross said, "but it's not necessary. We don't need to find Ludlow."

"We don't?" Victoria said. "Why not?"

Cross pointed to the message on the media wall. "Because he's coming for us."

Seth's phone rang. He picked it up.

"Yes?" Seth listened for a moment, nodded, then turned to Cross. "Senator Holbrook is here to see you."

The chairman of the Senate Intelligence Committee couldn't have picked a worse time for an unexpected visit. But Holbrook wouldn't have come for a face-to-face unless it was a high-priority issue.

"Send him to my office," Cross said.

Seth relayed the instruction as Cross walked out, slamming the door behind him. He took his time going down the corridor so he could get a grip on his anger and force the color out of his face. He reached his office door at the same moment as the portly senator, who smiled broadly when he saw Cross.

"Good morning, Will."

"I'm glad to see you in such a good mood, Senator." They shook hands and Cross opened his office door. "At least now I know you didn't come down here because of a crisis."

"That's not entirely true," Holbrook said, stepping into the room. "It's a national crisis, and your decisive handling of it, that brings me here."

Cross closed the door. "You can speak candidly. This office is totally secure."

"I would hope so," Holbrook said. "I just left the Oval Office. The president is very impressed with how you wrapped up this whole ugly business in less than forty-eight hours. It's phenomenal. You just bought him a second term."

"We're glad to be of service." Cross sat down in one of his guest chairs and Holbrook took the couch. The senator was so large that he needed the entire couch for himself.

"The president is going to show his appreciation by signing a classified executive order tonight giving Blackthorn control of the CIA's covert operations," Holbrook said. "Healy and the White House counsel will inform you in person when that happens."

The day hadn't gone totally to shit after all. "I'm surprised Healy is willing to do that."

"We're throwing him a big, fat carrot. The CIA and Belgian intelligence will share the credit for resolving this mess. Healy will resign in a few months as a national hero and Belgian intelligence won't be seen as a joke anymore. It's good politics, Will. You understand."

Cross didn't care who got the bragging rights. He got the personal glory of taking over the CIA and, in doing so, pulling off perhaps the greatest covert action in the history of espionage, not that anyone would know about it but him. At least during his lifetime. He could live with that.

"I'm only interested in what's best for our country," Cross said.

"I appreciate that, Will. The president will address the nation tomorrow morning, tell them that the skies are safe again and then he'll start bombing Syria into the Stone Age. That means more Pentagon business for you, too." Holbrook winked at Cross. "This is your lucky day."

Perhaps it was but right now what came to his mind were the words *fuck you* written in rubble in the wilds of Nevada.

⊕

Tarzana, California. July 21. 9:00 a.m. Pacific Standard Time.

In 1919, Edgar Rice Burroughs used the money that he'd made writing Tarzan books to buy a big spread in the San Fernando Valley that he named for the Lord of the Jungle. He called it Tarzana. But a few years later he got bored in the country, moved to Beverly Hills, and subdivided Tarzana. But the name stuck, even though there wasn't anything about the neighborhood that evoked the character or the books.

Ronnie had tried to change that. He bought a house in a Tarzana cul-de-sac, tore it down, and wanted to build in its place a massive tree house with rope vines that he could use for swinging around his jungle property in a loincloth. But his plans were shot down by uptight neighbors and a gutless planning commission. So Ronnie ended up building a typical Spanish Mediterranean McMansion with a lushly landscaped yard behind a high cinder-block wall topped with red ceramic tiles.

Margo pulled up to the gate, her front bumper nearly touching the elaborately curled and entwined wrought iron so Ronnie, sitting in the back seat, could roll down his window and reach out to the security keypad on a driver's side post. Beyond the gate, the cobblestone driveway curved up through immaculately maintained grounds to the mansion and its six-car garage.

Ronnie typed his code into the keypad. "Welcome to the house that *Frankencop* bought."

"*Frankencop?*" Margo said. "What is that?"

"A TV show," Ian said. "It ran for two seasons on Fox."

"*The best parts of twelve dead cops resurrected as one legendary hero,*" Ronnie intoned dramatically, performing the lines that played over the main titles. "The opening narration still moves me."

"Me too," Margo said. "It moves my breakfast right up my throat."

Ian peered out at the manicured lawns, perfectly trimmed trees, and blooming flower beds as the gate yawned open. "The place looks great. Why do you pay to maintain it if you don't live here anymore?"

"I have to maintain the property value. I don't trust banks or currency, because they're controlled by the New World Order so I keep a large percentage of my wealth in real estate."

"And the rest in doubloons," Margo added as she drove up to the house.

"I also come back here now and then for crucial supplies."

"Like what?" Ian asked.

"Wanda," Ronnie said. "LA is second only to Tokyo as the hotbed of the sex doll industry. Some dealers will even let preferred customers like me take the dolls out for a test drive. I can have one delivered in an hour."

"That's disgusting," Margo said.

But for Ian Ludlow, it was inspirational. Until that moment, Ian didn't have a plan. Now he did. The plot began to fall into place, fitting together like LEGO blocks. He didn't have the details yet, but he felt a familiar, reassuring rush of creative excitement. There was a book here and that meant there was a chance at salvation for him, Margo, and Ronnie.

They all got out of the car. Ronnie went to the door, unlocked it, and stepped inside, immediately setting off the alarm. He typed a code into the keypad by the door and deactivated the security system.

"Come on in," he said. "There are six bedrooms, six baths, two kitchens, a screening room, a wine cellar, and a six-car garage."

The grand entry was the center of the house. It was two stories high, encircled by the open second floor, and illuminated by sunshine streaming in from a skylight. All the other wings of the house branched off from the hall like spokes on a wheel. The interior was professionally decorated in a California hacienda style that was about as warm, personal, and inviting as a model home.

"The Carrara marble on the floor, and throughout the house, is from the same Tuscan quarry as the slab that Michelangelo used to carve the statue of *David*, who has the same body as me, except I have a much bigger schlong," Ronnie said. "Michelangelo said the statues were already in the rock—he just had to bring them out. So everywhere you go in this house you'll find the potential for greatness, and a big marble cock, all around you."

"That's a lot of money to pay for constant reassurance," Margo said.

"It's cheaper than seeing a shrink," Ronnie said.

"You should have seen the shrink instead." She checked her watch and turned to Ian. "Okay, time's up. Do you have a plan or not?"

Ian smiled. "I do."

And then he told her what it was.

CHAPTER THIRTY-SEVEN

The assassin Doric Thane arrived in Los Angeles tanned and thoroughly rested after his seven-day vacation in Hawaii. He'd practically had the entire island of Oahu to himself after he'd crashed the plane into Waikiki. The traumatized tourists couldn't wait to get off the island and the traumatized locals stayed indoors. He'd checked out of the Diamond Head hotel while Waikiki was still in flames and moved to a condo in sleepy Kailua, on the east end of the island, a mountain range between him and the devastation and chaos that he'd wrought. He spent his days swimming in the warm water, jogging on deserted beaches, and eating in empty restaurants. It was idyllic.

After arriving at LAX, he took a shuttle to the long-term parking lot, found his car, and drove to the Universal City Oakwood, a complex of furnished temporary-stay apartments on Barham Boulevard. The Oakwood was popular with businessmen, airline pilots and stewardesses, recently divorced fathers, and actors staying in LA for auditions, episodic guest shots, or movie shoots. Visiting assassins liked it, too.

The best part of staying there was the sex. Unless you had leprosy, it was almost impossible not to get laid. And even then, your chances were still pretty good.

The assassin hadn't been called into the office or given an assignment so he had time on his hands. Thane entered his apartment, changed into his Speedo, and went down to the pool, where there were several women sunbathing in bikinis for him to choose from. He picked a twentysomething who seemed to be posing for a nonexistent camera and was very proud of her new boobs. She had a right to be.

Thane stretched out on the chaise lounge next to hers, asked if he could steal some of her suntan lotion since he'd forgotten his and within two minutes he'd learned she was a stage actress from New York doing a guest shot on a cop show.

"I play an international hit woman," she said with a sly smile. "My body is a lethal weapon."

"Wow," Thane said. "Should I be scared?"

"Absolutely. When I play a part, I get under the character's skin. In the script, it says that she's a sociopath, that killing is the only thing that excites her, that she actually feels. That's bullshit. The writers have no clue who she is," the actress said, then leaned in close, as if sharing a dark secret. "Do you want to know what's really going on in an assassin's mind?"

"Beyond the preparation for the kill, and the escape afterward, they aren't thinking about anything at all," Thane said. "Taking a stranger's life is meaningless to them. It's a task to be performed, like a gardener pulling weeds."

She dismissed his remark with a wave of her hand, like she was swatting away a fly buzzing around her head. "That's completely wrong. Each time they kill someone, they're symbolically killing their parents, over and over, for the love they were denied. They're mourning their lost childhoods."

It was the stupidest thing he'd ever heard. He had a great relationship with his parents. They loved him unconditionally, though he wasn't tempted to test that belief by telling them that he'd hacked into an airplane and crashed it into Waikiki.

"That's fascinating," he said. "How do you know that?"

"I'm an actress," she said. "We instinctively find the emotional truth in a character."

"Does that work with real people, too?"

"Do you mean am I in tune with my own emotional truth?"

"No, I mean can you find mine?"

She smiled and stole a glance at his barely there Speedo and everything it strained to contain. "Definitely."

Bethesda, Maryland. July 21. 3:11 p.m. Eastern Standard Time.

"We got this from the Henderson Executive Airport parking lot," Seth said. "It shows the unknown subjects acquiring the Blackthorn vehicle that was left behind by Pessel and Bowers."

Cross watched pixelated video on the media wall of an old Ford station wagon pulling up beside the Suburban. Two men and a woman got out of the car but their faces weren't visible because the surveillance camera was crappy, it was too dark outside, and the people were too far away. But Cross didn't need to see their faces to know who they were. It was Ludlow, French, and one more civilian they'd have to kill.

"This gives us no useful intel," Cross said.

"Not by itself," Seth said. "But an identical 1974 Ford Country Squire station wagon was parked in the Main Street Station Casino parking lot, in direct line of sight of our Las Vegas office, at the time of the blast."

A video appeared on the media wall showing a rocket-propelled grenade being fired from the casino parking lot by someone obscured by the station wagon.

"That gave us a vehicle to search for," Seth said. "That same station wagon drove through the California agricultural checkpoint on I-15 at Yermo, a hundred and forty miles southwest of Las Vegas, at seven thirty-five a.m. Pacific Standard Time. It wasn't stopped for inspection but all the vehicles that go through are automatically photographed and the license plates are captured."

Seth put the two photos up on the media wall. One was a close-up of the rear license plate, which Cross didn't need or care to see. The second was a close-up of the front of the vehicle, heading toward the camera. It clearly showed Ian Ludlow sitting in the passenger seat and Margo French at the wheel.

Cross wanted to break Seth's neck. Seth should have immediately shown him the goddamn photo of Ian and Margo the instant he stepped into the room and scrapped the whole tedious story leading up to it. But no, Seth wanted to show off his work and build up suspense like he was putting on a fucking stage show. He'd wasted Cross' time and that was unacceptable. Cross would deal with that later. Maybe transfer the smug prick to Tasmania. For now, he took a deep breath to calm himself.

"Show me a map of the I-15 heading southwest," Cross said.

One appeared immediately on the media wall. The I-15 went straight into Southern California. The only fork beforehand was near Barstow, California, where the I-15 met the I-40 eastbound toward Arizona, New Mexico, and the lower third of the country. But if any of those places was their destination, there were much shorter routes out of Las Vegas to get there. So Cross was sure they'd stay on the I-15. Once they hit Victorville, they could take Highway 18 west, and from there hit several other routes heading to Central or Northern California. Or they could stay on the I-15 and connect to a number of southbound freeways toward San Diego and Mexico. Or they could take it straight into Los Angeles, Ian Ludlow's home.

"He's going back to Los Angeles," Cross said. He was sure of it, though it was just a gut feeling.

"He can't be," Victoria said. "That would be insane."

"More insane than breaking into our office in Las Vegas?" Seth said.

Victoria didn't reply. Seth had a point, Cross thought, and might even have the motive. Did Ludlow intend to strike their Beverly Hills office? Cross didn't think so. Ludlow wouldn't take the risk of returning to LA, his home and the place where he was most likely to be spotted by his pursuers, unless he absolutely had to for a crucial strategic or operational purpose.

"The real question is what's in Los Angeles that he needs?" Cross said, putting the question to the room.

"Money," Victoria said.

Cross nodded. That was a real possibility. But Ludlow wouldn't be dumb enough to walk into a bank or go to an ATM for a withdrawal. That would announce his location almost instantly. So that meant he had either money stashed away somewhere or someone he could approach for cash.

"Freeze his bank accounts and stake out his house, or what's left of it," Cross said. "Maybe he had a floor safe or something. Doesn't he have family in Southern California?"

"His mother is in Palm Springs," Victoria said.

"Put a team on her," Cross said. "I want her watched twenty-four/seven and all of her e-mail, phone, and other communications monitored. What did you get from the license plates on the station wagon?"

"It's owned by the same shell companies as the compound in Nevada," Seth said. "We're digging into it. We have our people sorting through records in Delaware, Panama, Bermuda, and the Cayman Islands. We're hours away from an answer."

"Make it minutes," Cross said.

And if Seth strung out the answer when he got it, Cross might actually break the man's neck.

CHAPTER THIRTY-EIGHT

Woodland Hills, California. July 21. 7:00 p.m. Pacific
Standard Time.

Margo parked the Ford station wagon in front of the Target store on Ventura Boulevard and looked at Ian in the passenger seat. He took the foil-wrapped driver's license out of his pocket.

"If you want to quit," Ian said, "now is the time to do it."

"No, I'm in."

"So you think the plan will work?"

"Not really. But it's how I choose to die." The sentence was barely out of her mouth before she started giggling like a little girl. "I don't know how you can write or say that Straker shit with a straight face."

"It's simple. You have to believe it."

He peeled the foil from his driver's license, gave her a smile, and got out of the car. She watched him walk into the Target and disappear inside.

Bethesda, Maryland. July 21. 10:17 p.m. Eastern Standard Time.

Cross sat in his office, watching CIA director Michael Healy's press conference, which was being aired live on every major TV network and cable news channel.

"Ayoub Darwish and Habib Ebrahimi, the two terrorists responsible for crashing TransAmerican 976 and, prior to that, Indonesian Air 230 were killed yesterday in Antwerp in a joint operation conducted by the CIA and Belgian intelligence," Healy said. "The two men have familial ties to Harakat Ahrar al-Sham al-Islamiyya, a coalition of radical Islamic terrorist groups based in Syria, and they worked on the Gordon-Ganza assembly line when both of the aircraft were manufactured. Evidence found on computers and cell phones recovered at the scene in Antwerp conclusively ties the men to the downing of those jets."

Poor Mike, Cross thought. It was his moment of glory, the kind of political coup that could easily propel a man of his youth to the Oval Office someday. Perhaps it would. But for now he had to stand there, freshly castrated, a Ken doll in a suit who had nothing to do until Cross or Holbrook or the president decided to play with him.

The Belgians were the luckiest bastards of all. They were given the shared glory for an intelligence coup they not only had nothing to do with but didn't know anything about until an hour or two before Healy's press conference. It was a gift, one that would allow them to downplay how Darwish and Ebrahimi were able to get into their country and remotely crash a plane in Honolulu from a barn outside of Antwerp, without Belgian intelligence knowing they were even there.

His phone rang and he snatched it up. "Yes?"

"Ludlow has surfaced." It was Victoria, calling from the control center.

"Where and when?"

"A Target store in Woodland Hills, California, thirty minutes ago. The alert in the national known shoplifter database paid off for us again. We got a hit from the RFID chip in his driver's license as he passed through the security scanners."

"I'll be right there."

When Cross entered the center, security camera video of Ludlow, taken from inside the Target store, was already playing on the media wall along with satellite images of the store and the surrounding neighborhood. There were also security camera photos from the parking lot showing Ludlow getting out of and into the old Ford station wagon.

"Do we know what Ludlow bought?" Cross asked.

"Four throwaway cell phones, hair coloring, toiletries, and groceries," Victoria said. "But all the food was packaged goods, nothing perishable like meat, fruit, or vegetables."

Ludlow was going into hibernation. If they lost him now, they might not have another shot at him until he made his next move against them. They had to take advantage of Ludlow's mistake while the opportunity was there.

"He's going back to ground, probably somewhere in Los Angeles," Cross said. "We have to move fast before we lose him. Get a surveillance drone up over the San Fernando Valley and try to home in on those RFID tags."

"He could be in Ventura by now," Victoria said. "Or halfway to Pasadena."

"I think I know where he is," Seth said. "The one common denominator of those shell companies and bank accounts is that they all lead back, through a lawyer or accountant, to Ronald Mancuso, an actor Ludlow worked with on the TV series *Hollywood & the Vine*." Publicity stills of Ronnie from his roles as Frankencop, Publicity Hound, and Charlie Vine appeared on the media wall. "Mancuso has a home in Tarzana, a few miles away from that Target store."

Seth didn't know it but he'd just saved himself from a one-way trip to Tasmania and the end of a once-promising career. Cross turned to Victoria. "Get me eyes on the house and dispatch a hit team."

"The asset we sent to Honolulu just got back to Los Angeles," Victoria said.

It was perfect timing and a good omen. Doric Thane was their best assassin and utterly dependable. It was why Cross had entrusted him with downing the plane.

"Put him in charge of the team and give him a helmet camera," Cross said. "I want to see Ludlow die for myself."

⊕

Ronnie led Ian and Margo into his garage and proudly showed off the six cars parked inside:

1.   The bright green 2011 Ford Crown Victoria from *Hollywood & the Vine*
2.   The black-and-gold 1977 Pontiac Trans Am from *Smokey and the Bandit*
3.   The red-and-white-striped 1976 Ford Gran Torino from *Starsky & Hutch*
4.   A silver 1964 Aston Martin DB5, like the one James Bond drove in *Goldfinger*
5.   KITT, the jet-black 1982 Pontiac Trans Am from *Knight Rider*
6.   The Batmobile from one of the Michael Keaton, Val Kilmer, or George Clooney string of *Batman* movies

Ronnie went over to the Batmobile and patted the hood. "I'm thinking this is the car for the job."

Ian went to the green Crown Vic, which had a set of ramming bars on the front grille, and gestured to it with a swing of the Target bag in his right hand. "Let's go with this one. It's a bit more subtle than the others."

"Not by much," Margo said.

"Do you know what this car is?" Ronnie asked her.

"Garish and ugly?"

"It's my ride from *Hollywood & the Vine*. Like the Batmobile, this car is rolling justice." Ronnie lovingly stroked the side of the Crown Vic and then nodded at Ian. "You're right, buddy. Driving this will make it personal."

"We don't have much time." Ian reached into his bag and handed a cell phone to Margo and another to Ronnie and kept the remaining two for himself. He looked Ronnie in the eye. "Are you sure you're okay with what might happen to you if this plays out the way we hope it will?"

"Absolutely," Ronnie said. "It's a small price to pay to topple the New World Order."

Ian gave him a hug. "I owe you."

"The hell you do," Ronnie said, still in Ian's embrace. "This is the fight I've always wanted. You've given me a gift, buddy."

Ian stepped back. "Then you better get going."

Ronnie held out his arms to Margo for another hug but she took a step back and offered him a friendly wave. "Good luck."

"Fuck luck, honey." Ronnie stuck the phone in his pocket. "I was born for this. See you at the after-party."

He got into the Crown Vic, used his remote to open the garage door, and drove out, burning rubber. Margo hit a button on the wall, closing the garage door. While she did that, Ian opened one of his two cell phones, typed *72, waited a moment, then began typing in a number with a 301 area code.

Margo joined him and looked over his shoulder. "Are you sure this is going to work?"

"Why are you asking me? It was basically your idea."

"It was never an idea," she said. "It was an example of something insane you could do to get yourself killed by the people who are chasing us."

"Uh-oh," he said. "I may have misunderstood."

"I hate you," she said and unpeeled the aluminum foil from her driver's license.

CHAPTER THIRTY-NINE

Studio City, California. 7:20 p.m. Pacific Standard Time.

The actress found the assassin's emotional truth after her second, bone-rattling orgasm.

"I know who you are," she said, catching her breath.

"You do?" Doric Thane lifted his face from between her legs and climbed up beside her on the bed. They'd hardly spoken since they'd met at the pool and even that didn't qualify as much of a conversation. He hadn't given her his name, not even a fake one, but she'd given him her full name and, when they arrived in her apartment, one of her head shots. Then she'd given him head.

Now she rolled over to face him, her body damp with sweat, her nipples hard enough to cut glass. "You're alone but not lonely. You are complete in yourself. Your pleasure comes from taking a job and doing it well but that's where your personal investment ends. Your emotional truth is that you don't have any emotions beyond pride in your work."

She'd been way off the mark on how an assassin thinks but Thane was impressed by how accurately she'd read him. "You got all that from how I fuck?"

"I'm guessing you're a surgeon."

Thane smiled. He liked that guess. "Why is that?"

"The way you handled my body and looked at me when I climaxed," she said. "It was like you were studying the response of individual muscles to your actions."

Right again. "Very observant."

His phone vibrated on her nightstand. Thane sat up, grabbed the phone, and looked at the screen. It was a text message telling him he was needed urgently at the office. That was code for a high-priority kill, one that had to be done immediately. He bent down and picked up his Speedo off the floor.

"I have to go." Thane stood and pulled on his Speedo in the same motion. "An emergency at the office."

He headed for the door.

"Wait, I have to know," she said, propping herself up on her elbows. "How close was I?"

He paused at her door, thought about his answer, and turned back to her. "I'm an exterminator."

She looked like she'd just eaten something sour. "You mean like rats and cockroaches?"

"It's always my parents." He walked out without taking her head shot.

The actress would go on to enjoy some fame two years later as the wacky neighbor with the beehive hairdo in the long-running CBS sitcom *Geez Louise*. But all four of her marriages would be destroyed by her adultery, a consequence of her futile quest to achieve the ecstasy that she'd experienced for three glorious hours with a stranger, a man she would never know was one of the biggest mass murderers in history.

Beverly Hills, California. July 21. 7:45 p.m. Pacific Standard Time.

Blackthorn occupied a sleek, eight-story monolith of black glass a few blocks west of Rodeo Drive. A ten-pound surveillance drone camouflaged to blend in with the sky lifted off from the top of the building. The drone had four helicopter-like propellers branching off from a central hub that held multiple high-definition cameras, an RFID scanner, and heat sensors. It circled once over the adjacent buildings, where Blackthorn snipers were keeping watch on the rooftops in case Ludlow attacked, and then it streaked out to the San Fernando Valley, the killing field.

Ronnie walked into the restroom of the Chevron station on Van Nuys Boulevard but twenty minutes later it was Detective Charlie Vine who walked out. He wore a cheap suit and had a badge clipped to his belt. His hair was vibrant green and matched the color of his Crown Vic. He got into the car and sped off, the theme from *Hollywood & the Vine* blasting from his stereo.

> Ooooh you heard about that cop Vine
> A plant who can't stand crime
> You get caught, you're gonna do time . . .
> Honey, honey yeah . . .

In the basement armory of Blackthorn's Beverly Hills office, Doric Thane and five other men suited up in their black tactical gear and prepared for battle. They wore ballistic helmets with cameras, night-vision goggles, armored vests, kneepads, and duty belts loaded with stun grenades, pepper spray, doorstops, flashlights, and extra magazines and rounds of ammunition. They were armed with knives, Sig Sauer P226 semiautomatic pistols, and Heckler & Koch HK416 assault rifles with suppressors and mounted lights.

Doric Thane thought that killing by laptop, with a cocktail in your hand, was a lot easier on the lower back than carrying all of this but it wasn't nearly as much fun.

A flat-screen TV on the wall displayed pictures of their three targets: Ian Ludlow, Margo French, and Ronald Mancuso. Wilton Cross' voice came through on the speaker, giving them their marching orders.

"This is a stealth operation, swift and quiet. The targets are well trained and heavily armed. They have already killed three of our agents, shot down one of our helicopters, and bombed our Las Vegas offices. Don't underestimate them. Kill them on sight. Leave no witnesses."

"Roger that," Thane said.

He led the men out of the armory and into the underground garage, where they split up, got into the two waiting black panel vans, and raced out of the building.

Some clichés are true. Cops really *do* love doughnuts and coffee. That's especially true for California Highway Patrol officers. That's because doughnut shops offer a cheap, quick fix of sugar and caffeine, they're open all hours, and they can usually be found within two blocks of any freeway off-ramp in Los Angeles County.

Rolley's Donuts, where CHP officers Brubeck and Flotz were taking a break, was a good example. It was one block south of the Coldwater Canyon off-ramp of the 101 freeway and there was almost always a police car parked in the lot. This time it was their black-and-white CHP Ford Explorer.

Flotz held his glazed old-fashioned doughnut in front of his face and pondered its beauty and complexity. "Doughnuts are an American delicacy."

"You bet. Right up there with fried chicken and barbecue ribs." Brubeck slurped some of his coffee. He and his partner were both in their midthirties, as pale as vampires from working nights, and one belt-buckle notch away from having to buy wider pants.

They sat at a window table along the street. They weren't paying attention to the parking lot or the alley behind it. Neither one of them noticed the green Crown Vic that pulled up behind the dumpsters. If they had, they probably would have mistaken it for a cop driving a plain wrap, coming in for a break.

"So why is it that Koreans make the best doughnuts?" Flotz gestured to the Korean woman who sat on a stool behind the counter, reading a Korean-language newspaper.

"The doughnuts in this place have been terrific for forty-seven years," Brubeck said, "long before Fat Rolley retired and sold the place to Ho Chi Minh."

"That's Vietnamese. I'm talking about Koreans."

"My point is that the Koreans, the Vietnamese, and other Asians bought up all the old mom-and-pop doughnut shops and the recipes came with the deal," Brubeck said. "What they're good at is following recipes."

Flotz took a bite and savored it. "I bet if an American bought the place, the doughnuts would taste like shit—that's *my* point."

The Crown Vic slammed into the trash bin, the sound of the crash immediately getting the attention of the two cops. They turned around just as the Crown Vic bulldozed the bin right into the driver's side of their Explorer, T-boning it.

"What the fuck?" Brubeck said.

The Crown Vic backed up, tires squealing, and then charged forward again, plowing into the bin and pushing the Explorer through the plate-glass window of the doughnut shop.

Brubeck and Flotz ducked for cover from the flying glass. They drew their weapons and stood up to see a man with green hair in the driver's seat of the Crown Vic, waving at them as he sped into traffic on Coldwater Canyon. Both cops took aim but neither could get a clear shot without hitting other passing cars. The Crown Vic fishtailed as it made a sharp turn south toward Ventura Boulevard.

Flotz grabbed the radio clipped on his shoulder and called in the cavalry.

The media wall showed a drone's-eye view of Ronnie's house and the Ford station wagon parked in the motor court. A separate video window opened up on the wall, showing the layout of the house and two red pulses upstairs. Those were good signs.

Victoria spoke up, sharing information from her computer screen. "The drone is getting positive RFID hits on Ludlow's driver's license, French's driver's license, and the Target purchases. We also have two heat signatures upstairs."

It was almost certain that Ludlow and French were in the house. But the third man, the actor, could be anywhere. Cross frowned. There would still be a Rogue Element left after Ludlow and French were finally off the field. This was the fuckup that never stopped giving.

"We've hacked into the house's surveillance camera system through a back door in their ancient router," Seth said. "We've disabled the alarms and we've recorded the last sixty seconds of footage of the grounds. We are rerunning it in a loop in case anyone inside the house is watching the monitors. They won't see what's coming."

Cross turned to Victoria. "ETA?"

"Five minutes," she said.

CHAPTER FORTY

The first thing that Margo did when she and Ian walked into the bedroom was turn on the TV to the local news. The lead story was live coverage of a high-speed police chase on the westbound Ventura Freeway, which was less than a block north of Ronnie's house and ran parallel to the boulevard.

They stood in front of the TV set and stared at the video from the Channel 2 news chopper. It showed Ronnie's bright green Crown Vic illuminated by a spotlight from an LAPD helicopter and being pursued by four CHP patrol cars.

"At least the green paint job makes the car easy to spot from the air," Margo said, taking out her cell phone and beginning to dial.

"I'm glad you're seeing the positive side of things." Ian said and went to the next room. He also had a call to make and he didn't want to hear the TV.

◎

Ronnie's house backed up against a lightly wooded hillside that was owned by the county. A private road led up the hill to an eight-million-gallon water tank, the gravel lot around it the romantic spot where hundreds, if not thousands, of teenagers over the last forty years had drunk their first beer, inhaled their first joint, and lost their virginity, making it worthy by Los Angeles standards of historic preservation and a brass plaque. Like actresses, anything over forty that was still standing in Los Angeles was considered ancient.

A Blackthorn van rolled up the county road with its lights off and parked above Ronnie's property. The three killers got out, rifles drawn, and moved methodically down the hillside, wary of any hidden threats.

At the same time, the other Blackthorn van arrived in front of the house. Thane and two of his men spilled out, climbed on top of the van, and from there they easily scaled Ronnie's wall and dropped down silently on the other side.

Thane and his men advanced on the house, ready to engage the enemy, at the same time the other team closed in from the rear.

◎

The attention of every operative in the Blackthorn situation room was on the media wall, which was split into thirds. The first third showed the point of view from Thane's camera helmet as he led his team toward the house. The second showed the drone's night-vision-camera view of the property and the six men who were approaching the house from the front and the rear. The last third showed the drone's heat-sensor display of the property, tracking the six men closing in on the house, and the two people in bedrooms on the second floor.

"Any activity in the neighborhood?" Cross asked. "Any calls to the police?"

"All quiet," Seth said. "And even if there were, the police are occupied with a pursuit on the Ventura Freeway."

"A police pursuit is daily news in Los Angeles, like the weather or sports," Victoria said.

"Thank you, O.J.," Seth said.

Cross nodded to himself, pleased. Finally, luck was on their side.

Ronnie's car was bathed in the police chopper's spotlight as he weaved through the moderate freeway traffic toward the White Oak exit. The news chopper's cameraman kindly gave Margo a wide-angle view of what lay ahead for Ronnie. She could see two lines of cars stacked up at the White Oak exit because of a red light at the bottom of the off-ramp.

"Don't use the White Oak exit," Margo warned Ronnie on the phone. "There's a backup and you'll get pinned. The next exit at Reseda looks clear."

She could hear an action-adventure, percussion-heavy, instrumental version of "I Heard It Through the Grapevine" playing on his car stereo.

"Gotcha," Ronnie said as he passed the White Oak off-ramp. "But I have a better idea, Hollywood."

"Don't call me that," she said. "This is not a TV show."

But that wasn't entirely true. She was watching him on TV and as she spoke he made a sharp U-turn on the freeway and headed down the White Oak on-ramp. It was an insane car-chase stunt worthy of prime time.

Ronnie charged down the shoulder, narrowly avoiding collisions with oncoming cars and scraping the wall along the edge of the embankment, then made a hard right southbound onto White Oak, nearly clipping a bus making the turn onto the on-ramp.

"Woo-wee!" Ronnie roared.

The bold, propulsive music he was playing was the perfect score for the action. For a moment, she almost forgot that she was watching live TV and not a *Hollywood & the Vine* rerun.

"Oh my God," the anchorman said. "The driver is a lunatic."

The anchorman's astute observation snapped Margo back to reality, or at least what was passing for it lately. Ronnie's car disappeared briefly from the chopper's view under the freeway overpass, then reappeared speeding south toward Ventura Boulevard.

"You thought going the wrong way down a freeway on-ramp was a better idea than simply taking the next exit?" Margo said.

"It was definitely more fun," Ronnie said. "It was also the unpredictable thing to do, which is always the right choice if you don't want to get caught."

"You could get yourself and a lot of other people killed," she said. "I know you're fleeing from the police but you can do it responsibly."

"Loosen up, Hollywood. You're stiffer than my uncle Oak and he's a tree."

⊕

Cross watched the assault from Doric Thane's POV as the assassin and his two men entered Ronnie's brightly lit house and moved into the entry hall, which was a two-story atrium with a staircase on the far end. It was a big space, open to the second floor. The three men were completely exposed. If an ambush was coming, it would be here and now. Ludlow and French, armed with AK-47s, could mow them all down from above or drop a couple of hand grenades and splatter them on the walls.

Thane's men were well aware of their vulnerability. They pointed their weapons up, covering their leader as he made his way to the stairs. It was very tense and everyone was silent in the situation room.

Cross' phone vibrated in his jacket, startling him. Nobody called him on this phone unless it was priority Blackthorn business. What could be more important than what was happening right now? There could be a crisis somewhere involving a major client, like one of the third-world dictators they were propping up. Or perhaps it was something involving the president's imminent secret executive order. As much as he wanted to, he couldn't ignore the call. He took the phone out of his pocket and answered it.

"Cross," he said.

"Hello, Willie. This is Ian. I understand you've been looking for me."

Ian's voice hit Cross like a gut punch. This call was the ambush. It had to be. But what was the trap? He didn't know if the call was being recorded or broadcast so he'd have to choose his words wisely. Cross snapped his fingers to get Victoria's attention and replied more loudly to Ian than he needed to.

"I just wanted to express how much I enjoy your spy thrillers, Mr. Ludlow, even if they are a bit far-fetched."

The instant Victoria heard Ludlow's name, she got the message to trace the call and she urgently typed commands on her keyboard.

"But lately my stories have been so true to life, don't you think, Willie?" Ian said. "Like that plane crash in Honolulu, for example. It's almost as if I've written the day's news myself."

CHAPTER FORTY-ONE

Ronnie drove westbound in the eastbound lanes of Ventura Boulevard, straight into oncoming traffic, pursued by a posse of police cars, their sirens wailing and lights flashing to warn drivers about what was coming at them. He swerved around the oncoming cars, occasionally drifting into the center turning lane, then back into traffic again. The stunned TV anchor team, a man and a woman, and their Sky 2 chopper pilot provided ongoing commentary, frequently stating the obvious just to fill the airtime.

"Wayne, is that a spike strip they are laying down?" the anchorwoman asked the pilot. "I see some activity in the top corner of the screen."

The chopper's camera view shifted from Ronnie for a moment to the road ahead and zoomed in. The police had blocked traffic at the intersection with Reseda Boulevard and were laying a spike stripe across Ventura Boulevard in both directions.

"Yes, it is, Trixie," the chopper pilot said. "This is a very dangerous driver who has to be stopped."

He would be, too, if he didn't have Margo watching out for him. She spoke into the phone. "They've put a spike strip down across all the lanes at Reseda."

In response, Ronnie made a sudden, hard left onto a residential side street. One of the police cars tried to follow him and clipped a truck, sending both vehicles spinning and causing a chain reaction pileup.

"Yee-haw," Ronnie yelled, leaving the destruction in his wake, but not his pursuers. The police cars at the Reseda intersection quickly peeled off, joining the chase. One LAPD chopper and three from local TV news stations also followed him overhead. And, according to ratings released by the Nielsen Company the following week, eight hundred thousand Los Angelenos were watching him, too.

⊕

Doric Thane reached the top of the stairs, his two men behind him, covering his back. The second team remained outside, guarding the perimeter in case the targets tried to escape. But the intel Thane got in his earpiece from the Blackthorn situation room confirmed that Ludlow and French were still in the two bedrooms at the end of the hall. And the surveillance drone circling the house was still sensing their body heat and pinging their driver's licenses. The drone even sensed that the Ding Dongs, potato chips, and dry salami that they bought at Target were still in the kitchen. All that remained to do was kill them and grab a Ding Dong for the road.

⊕

"I wouldn't be surprised if you were in the news yourself tomorrow," Cross said to Ian. On the media wall, he could see Thane's slow advance down the hall toward an open bedroom door.

"That's why I'm calling," Ian said. "To let you know how my latest thriller ends and what tomorrow's news will be."

Victoria got up from her seat and handed a note to Cross.

He's calling from the house.

Cross smiled at her and replied to Ian: "I think I may already know the ending."

⊕

Thane burst into the bedroom, saw a woman in a negligee on the bed, and shot her three times before he even had a good look at her. The first bullet punctured her head and popped out her left eyeball. The other two rounds disappeared into the cleavage between her huge breasts. A split second after he pulled the trigger he noticed the troubling absence of brain and blood splatter. In the next instant, he saw the electrical cord running from her back to a wall plug and the glass eyeball rolling across the hardwood floor to his feet and knew he was in deep shit.

The stunned operatives in the Blackthorn situation room, however, had a good long look at her before, during, and after the shooting.

"Is that . . . *a sex doll?*" Seth asked.

⊕

"A hit team closes in on the one man who can reveal that a private security company hacked into a jet and crashed it into Waikiki," Ian said. "Are you with me, Willie?"

Cross stared at the media wall and tried to understand what he was seeing. Thane went to the bed for a closer look. The woman had a provocative, slightly bemused expression on her face that took on a new meaning with the hole in her forehead and the empty eye socket. Instead of saying "Fuck me," her expression now seemed to be saying "Fuck you."

On the bed beside the woman, and her humming crotch, was Margo French's driver's license. Thane abruptly turned to the door, where his two men stood, looking lost.

"Out of my way," Thane said.

The men parted and Thane marched into the next bedroom, where a male sex doll in a used business suit from Goodwill lay on the bed, his enormous hard-on poking out of his open fly, a throwaway cell phone in his hand. There was no ambiguity about the message this sex doll was expressing. It was clearly, indisputably, "Fuck you."

Bile rose in Cross' throat and he forced it down with a hard swallow.

"Your story is outlandish," Cross said, hearing the shakiness in his voice. "Nobody will believe it."

"Nobody has to believe it and I don't have to make a case," Ian said. "That's the beauty of the big twists that are coming."

Cross glanced at Victoria, who was as perplexed as he was. She pointed to the big screen.

"That's definitely the phone that's calling you," she said. "Ludlow should be on that bed."

Seth started to laugh, more out of barely contained hysteria than any amusement. "It's call forwarding. He's calling that phone from somewhere else and it's forwarding the call to us."

⊕

The shocked silence from Cross sounded wonderful to Ian, who sat with a big grin on his face in his room at the Tarzana Resort Motel on Ventura Boulevard, a safe distance away from Ronnie's house.

"The first twist is that the man they're trying to kill isn't there," Ian said. "But you already know that. Are you ready for the second twist?"

In the adjoining room, Margo watched on TV as Ronnie's car charged into a cul-de-sac.

"It's over for this guy now," the anchorman said. "There's nowhere for him to go."

That wasn't entirely true, because it was Ronnie's house at the end of the cul-de-sac. Ronnie smashed through the gate and charged up to the front door, bringing along a dozen police cars, four helicopters, and a viewing audience of eight hundred thousand people.

The spotlight from the LAPD helicopter exposed three black-clad commandos with automatic weapons who were positioned around the house.

"Who are those guys?" the anchorman asked. "And why are they holding rifles?"

Thane shot the penis off the sex doll out of pure anger as the house shook from the rumble of helicopters overhead, the sound of their rotors almost drowning out the sirens and the desperate chatter in his earbud from his men outside.

They were all fucked. There was only one command he could give to his men and it was laughably obvious. But he gave it anyway.

"Get the hell out of here!"

And as he rushed out of the room and down the stairs, his two men right behind him, he added one more command: "No surrender!"

But Thane wondered, as he ran down the stairs, if they would really die fighting to avoid capture, prosecution, and punishment, not necessarily for this trespass, but for all of the killing they'd done before. And they'd all done a *lot* of killing, though not as much as him, not after Honolulu. Only a few people in history could top his record, and most of them were dead.

His men might not go down fighting but he would. Thane would not be tried, imprisoned, or executed. He would go down in glory, the kind befitting a man of his professionalism and deadly accomplishment, in a gun battle with other trained killers, which was what any law enforcement officer or soldier really was.

Thane yanked open the front door, prepared to face a firing line of police, but not for the surreal sight that confronted him.

A man with wild green hair leaped out of a green Crown Vic and, illuminated in the sixty thousand lumens of harsh white light from the helicopter above, snatched the badge from his belt and held it up for Thane to see.

"Charlie Vine, LAPD," the green man said. "You're nipped in the bud, scumbag."

It was an obscene joke, a horrific indignity, and Thane deserved so much better. He screamed in unbridled rage and pointed his HK416 assault rifle at the green clown and just as his finger began to squeeze the trigger, the two dozen cops hidden in the blackness behind the spotlight's glare opened fire.

CHAPTER FORTY-TWO

Wilton Cross saw it all. The police. The news choppers. The brief gun battle that ended with the death of all but two of his men, who dropped their weapons and surrendered.

"The twist is that the hit team is caught in the act by the police," Ian said in his ear. "On live television."

It wasn't the first time Cross had been tricked, outmaneuvered, and humiliated. But before it had always been covert, playing out in some dark corner of the globe, and known only within the shadow world of international espionage. Never like this, witnessed by dozens of cops and a live television audience. Within minutes, it would go global, if it hadn't already. This would be on every newscast in every country on earth and all over the Internet. It was an unimaginable disaster. There would be no way to bury this or cover it up.

Everyone in the situation room stared at the media wall in shock as the nightmare continued to unfold. The image was so big, it was like they were right in the middle of it, too.

The police, their guns drawn, closed in on Ronnie, who put his hands on his head and dropped to his knees as ordered. He was quickly forced to the ground, handcuffed, and then escorted to a black-and-white. In the midst of that, nobody noticed Cross slip out of the room with the phone to his ear. Or, if they did, they wisely ignored it, not wanting to look at their boss and see his fury or his profound humiliation.

"But here's the beauty of it," Ian said into Cross' ear. "The hero doesn't have to tell his unbelievable story. The bad guys have done the job for him. They've taken themselves down. The investigation resulting from their actions will reveal the whole shocking conspiracy."

Cross knew that Ludlow was absolutely right. It wouldn't take long for the investigation in Los Angeles to lead back to Blackthorn and, eventually, to him. There would be years of trials and Senate hearings, dozens of arrests and indictments, and a scandal that would permanently damage the CIA, the presidency, and the nation, all of which he'd spent his life protecting.

Cross entered his office and sat at his desk.

"I think it's a very credible, relevant story of corruption, greed, and political arrogance that could easily happen today and be in the news tomorrow," Ian said. "What do you think?"

Cross sighed, feeling oddly relaxed after the heightened anxiety he'd felt only moments ago. The game was over and he'd lost. All he could do now was attempt to lessen the damage but it would still be catastrophic.

"This is why we don't have anyone with imagination in the intelligence business," Cross said. "It's too dangerous."

"Imagination isn't what's dangerous," Ian said. "It's people like you."

"People like me are the ones who make the sacrifices and tough decisions necessary to keep America safe."

"Is that what you did for the people on TransAmerican Flight 976 and in Waikiki?" Ian said. "What have you sacrificed, Willie, that can match what they lost?"

Cross' desk phone rang and the line button lit up that indicated that the call was from the receptionist at the front desk. He set his cell phone down on his blotter, picked up the telephone receiver, and answered the call.

"Yes?" he said.

"Director Healy and Ms. Jones are here to see you, sir," the receptionist said.

"Send them in."

Cross hung up and sat there for a moment, considering his options and anticipating possible outcomes, a strategist to the end. There was a knock at the door.

"Come in," Cross said.

Healy strode in, his forced smile making him look nauseated. Cross couldn't blame him if he was. At his side was Loretta Jones, a statuesque African American woman who, before pursuing a career in law that led her to the White House, was an exceptional long-distance runner eyed as a potential Olympic medalist. She held a leather binder under her arm that was embossed with the presidential seal.

"Sorry for intruding so late. I take it you know Loretta Jones, the White House counsel?" Healy said. Cross nodded. "She has an executive order to read to you."

"You will not be given a copy, for obvious reasons," she said. "But if details or the scope of the order are ever in question, you or your counsel can contact me directly for clarification."

"I can't say I'm happy about this, Will," Healy said. "But I can't argue with success."

Cross smiled at that and opened his desk drawer. "Especially when you get all the credit for it, Mike."

"You're getting something out of it, too," Healy said.

"I certainly am." Cross took the Glock out of the drawer, put the muzzle under his chin, and pulled the trigger.

Two thousand six hundred thirty-six miles away, in a motel room in Tarzana, Ian Ludlow sat bolt upright, staring at his phone like it was a live cobra. He'd heard every word and, of course, the gunshot.

The conversation that he'd heard, while he didn't know what it all meant, could potentially make him a target again and this time it really *would* be the CIA that was after him.

But he wasn't ready to hang up yet. He had to know what had happened.

Healy's ears were ringing but his mind was racing, trying to make sense of what had just happened. The top of Cross' head was gone, smeared all over the wall behind him. Why would Cross kill himself at his moment of triumph?

Jones turned her back to the desk, bent over, and took a deep breath, struggling to maintain her composure. She wasn't accustomed to violence. After a long moment, she straightened up, tugged at her pantsuit, and, without looking back at Healy or the gruesome scene, said just four words: "We were never here."

Healy knew that every instinct Jones had was telling her to run away as fast as she could, which was Olympic-gold-medal fast, but she didn't. Instead, she marshaled all of her resolve and walked calmly out of the office as if she were leaving a routine meeting. But there hadn't been anything routine about this from the moment the president had her draft the secret order, which Healy knew Jones had strongly advised against. In fact, she probably should have drafted her resignation instead of the secret order. Healy was certain that she'd write that letter tonight and get the hell out of the White House before this president could take her down with him.

Healy didn't respond to Jones nor did he watch her go. His gaze had drifted to the iPhone on Cross' desk at the same instant that CALL ENDED appeared on the screen. Someone had heard it all.

Ian had now witnessed two violent deaths. At least he didn't have to see this one with his own eyes. But his ear was still ringing. He took the SIM card out of the phone and broke it in half. They wouldn't be able to trace the call back to him and he'd keep his mouth shut. He'd let the story play out exactly the way he'd pitched it to Cross. He hoped that would keep him and Margo out of this. He knew Ronnie wasn't going to say anything. And perhaps the only other person who knew about Ian's involvement in all of this, the asshole Cross, had just killed himself. Ian was cautiously optimistic that the nightmare was over.

Margo rushed into the bedroom. She was very excited and speaking fast.

"The hit team is down and Ronnie is fine, even though he was standing right in the middle of a gunfight. It worked just like you plotted it, more or less. Ronnie couldn't stop himself from improvising, of course, and it almost got him killed but I guess you're used to actors who stray from the script." She stopped, noticing the distress on Ian's face. "What's wrong?"

"I think Cross either killed himself or was murdered while I was talking to him."

"What do you mean, you 'think'?"

"I heard him talking to two people, then the gunshot and a woman said, 'We were never here.'"

"Who was in the room?"

He knew it was the acting director of the CIA and the White House counsel delivering some kind of executive order from the president that gave something big to Blackthorn. And, from what he'd heard, Healy wasn't too happy about it. Whatever the executive order was, it took things to a new, very scary level of dark shit and Ian wanted nothing to do with it. But his mind was already whirling with the creative possibilities.

"It's better for you if you don't know," Ian said. "I wish I didn't."

"But if Cross is dead, and we know after tonight that Blackthorn is going down, it means it's over, right?" she said. "We can stop running."

"Yes, it does," Ian said.

"Holy crap," she said. "We actually won!"

Margo threw herself into Ian's arms and gave him a big, enthusiastic kiss. He lost his balance and tumbled backward onto the double bed, Margo landing on top of him. She kissed him again. Ian wasn't certain but there was a strong possibility he was in love. He was definitely aroused.

"You're wonderful," she said.

"So now you have a big surprise for me."

"I do?"

"You're going to tell me that you aren't really gay," he said. "You just weren't attracted to me yet."

"No, I'm a lesbian."

"But you're going to switch teams so you can have me. After this experience, you feel this deep, unbreakable bond with me and can't imagine us ever being apart."

"Nope," she said, getting off him. "Still gay and looking forward to getting far away from you and the terror you brought into my life."

"Well," he said. "That's definitely going to change in the book."

CHAPTER FORTY-THREE

Nobody in the Blackthorn building heard Wilton Cross shoot himself because, as a security precaution, he'd had his office soundproofed. That gave Healy plenty of time to consider the situation and take action. He was certain that the suicide was a spontaneous, desperate act. The only reason Cross, or any spy, would take that last resort would be to keep his secrets safe in the face of certain capture. That meant something had just gone catastrophically wrong that imperiled Blackthorn and, Healy assumed, the impending classified arrangement with the CIA. The priority now was finding out what had happened and whatever it was that Cross wanted to hide by taking his life.

Healy took out his phone and called Cotter, the leader of his four-man personal protection unit, which was waiting outside with his bulletproof SUV.

"Has the White House counsel left?" Healy asked.

"Yes, sir," Cotter said. "Her car is leaving now. In fact, judging by how fast she's going, she's in a big hurry to get somewhere."

"As soon as she's out of sight, secure the building. Do not allow anyone to leave. Use deadly force if necessary," Healy said. "A containment squad will be here shortly to relieve you."

Healy disconnected and called the CIA situation room. Norman Kelton answered on the first ring.

"Yes, sir?" Kelton said, not waiting for introductions. The blue phone that he'd answered was for the exclusive use of the director of the CIA.

"We need to lock down Blackthorn's headquarters in Bethesda immediately. Take everything and everyone and then scrub the place afterward. The employees are to be held and treated as enemy agents until proven otherwise. Bring in our best interrogators. I will brief them shortly."

Kelton didn't question the commands. Healy wouldn't order the deployment of an armed force to Blackthorn, the seizure of all their equipment and files, the apprehension and interrogation of their personnel, and a forensic cleansing of the scene unless a serious security breach had occurred and someone had been killed. This sort of mission was often done overseas, particularly when invading an enemy's headquarters. The fact that he'd ordered it on US soil, where the CIA was not authorized to operate, only underscored the severity of the situation and the danger to national security.

"The containment squad will be there in ten minutes," Kelton said.

Healy disconnected. His men would arrive in a fleet of vehicles from a fictitious emergency fire-and-water-damage cleanup company. It was an appropriate cover.

He opened the door just wide enough to allow him to step out of the office and came face-to-face with an Asian woman who'd been on her way in, startling them both. It was clear from her expression that she recognized him. She would suck at her job if she didn't. She took a step back and he pulled the door fully closed behind him.

"Excuse me, sir," she said. "I was on my way in to see Mr. Cross."

"He's busy on an urgent national security matter," Healy said. "And you are?"

"Victoria Takahara," she said. "Vice president of global operations, sir."

He nodded. "Ms. Takahara, I have to ask you and your colleagues to remain in the building until you can be briefed on this rapidly unfolding, highly classified situation. In the meantime, I need you to tell your colleagues not to communicate with anyone outside of this building by any means. Do you understand?"

"Yes, sir," she said. "I'll let the others know."

"Thank you, I'd appreciate that."

Victoria continued down the hall and went to her office. She hadn't seen inside Cross' office but there was no mistaking the smell of warm brain matter. It was an unforgettable scent. Given the events of the last hour, and the CIA lockdown of the building, she had a pretty clear idea of what was about to unfold and what she had to do before the containment team got here.

She went to her desk, took out her Glock and two extra, loaded magazines, and stuck the gun in her pants and covered it with her jacket. She put the magazines in her pocket, grabbed a letter opener off her desk, stuck it in her pants, too, and walked out again.

Victoria returned to the situation room, closed the door behind her, and locked it. The thirty operatives in the room were still captivated by the catastrophe in Los Angeles that was unfolding on the media wall.

Seth turned to her. "What did Cross say?"

She looked past him and shouted to the room: "Attention, everyone. Code Red. I repeat, Code Red."

Victoria didn't have to say more. This was a carefully rehearsed disaster protocol and everyone knew what they had to do. Frenzy swept the room as operatives frantically typed commands to erase their computers and, as their electronic files were being deleted, began brushing the papers off their desks into burn bags.

An operative hurried through the room, collecting the burn bags and taking them to a large metal bin that Seth wheeled out of a utility closet. The bags each contained a small amount of thermite, a powdered mixture of aluminum and iron oxide that created molten metal when ignited, to guarantee a hot burn. Once all the bags were in the bin, Seth used a gun-shaped butane barbecue lighter to set the bags on fire. The flames erupted almost instantly, startling Seth and nearly scorching him.

The media wall went dark, deprived of the data that kept it alive and so did every computer screen. The whole operation to scrub the room, and effectively Blackthorn itself on a global level, from incriminating data took three minutes.

That's when Victoria, from her high position in the back of the room, began calmly firing her Glock. She shot Seth first, hitting him between the eyes. He slumped over the edge of the bin and immediately caught on fire. She methodically picked off one person after another. Some people got head shots, others she shot in the knees just to take them down. It was easy pickings. They were all unarmed and had no place to hide.

But a few of them were trained soldiers. When she ejected her first empty magazine, one man tried to charge her but she stabbed him in the throat with the letter opener, jammed a fresh magazine in her Glock, and kept firing until she was certain that everyone was either dead or too badly wounded to get out alive.

By then, flames had engulfed the media wall, the fire alarm was wailing, the sprinklers on the ceiling were spraying, and there were people outside in the hallway pounding on the door. She wasn't concerned by the water or the people trying to get in. The water wouldn't douse the thermite-fed blaze, and the situation room door was designed to withstand explosives. She had plenty of time to make sure all the evidence was destroyed before she removed the last piece, which was herself.

CHAPTER FORTY-FOUR

The naked woman on the metal exam table in the center of the windowless room looked like a burned mannequin. The contrast of her blackened body against the white walls and harsh light intensified for Healy the visual impact of her horrific charring. There was little about her that identified her as human except for her mewling and, as Healy stepped closer, the few patches of skin that he could see on her face, neck, and shoulders that had been spared the touch of flame. The countless tubes entering her body kept her alive and conscious but were doing very little to reduce her agony. Those were Healy's orders. He wanted her alert and in misery.

She was the only surviving operative from Blackthorn's situation room. She'd been shot in the kneecaps and left to burn by Victoria Takahara, who'd subsequently blown her own head off. But this operative had managed to drag herself through the flames into the utility closet where the trash bin and burn bags had been kept. The firefighters found her barely alive, but just enough for Healy's needs. He'd had her brought back to the CIA's secret medical facility at Langley for a little chat, though she'd already been declared among the Blackthorn dead as far as the public and her family were concerned.

He pulled up a metal chair beside her. She smelled like a burned steak marinated in piss. Her eyes were open and locked on him. He had no sympathy for her because he suspected what she'd been a part of. Healy had given a lot of thought to what might have motivated Cross to take his own life on the verge of attaining total control of all of the CIA's covert operations, an unbelievable coup that wouldn't have happened if not for the crash of TransAmerican 976. The sequence of events was not lost on him. But he needed proof.

"The body is like a water balloon," Healy whispered into her toasted ear. "Your skin is the only thing holding in all the fluid and, let's face it, most of your skin is gone. The life is oozing out of you. And since you're basically skinless, you've got no protection against infection. Your exposed organs are being ravaged by germs. We haven't bothered removing the bullets from your knees because there's no point. You're never getting off this table, except to be put into a body bag. All of these tubes in your body will extend your life to the last possible second and keep you conscious, and in a constant state of unbearable, excruciating agony, until massive organ failure finally kills you. It might only be a day, or perhaps two, but for you it will feel like an eternity. That might seem cruel, perhaps even inhuman, but we both know that you deserve it, don't we?"

Tears ran out of the woman's eyes, which Healy found surprising, given how little moisture she had to spare.

"Or we can pump you so full of painkillers and other drugs that you'll believe you're living in Candyland until the end comes and you'll die a peaceful, painless death," Healy said. "It's your choice. Give me a reason to show you some mercy. Tell us what Takahara was trying to cover up and you get Candyland. Keep quiet and you experience the worst death imaginable."

"You don't have to threaten me." Her voice was weak and raspy. It sounded like each word that she spoke was serrated and cut the back of her throat on the way out. She wouldn't be able to talk for long. "Victoria killed us all to hide what we did. I want to look that bitch in the eye in hell and tell her that she failed."

"What did Blackthorn do?"

"We crashed an airplane into Waikiki," she said.

⊕

Capitol Hill, Washington, DC. July 24. 10:00 a.m. Eastern Standard Time.

Acting CIA director Michael Healy sat at the table in front of the seven stony-faced senators in the hearing room and, having verbally shared the details of his investigation into the Blackthorn matter, was about to deliver the conclusion of his classified report. There would be no written copies, for obvious reasons, and he would be destroying his notes at the end of his unrecorded testimony.

"There was no foreign terrorist conspiracy behind the crash of TransAmerican 976 and Ayoub Darwish and Habib Ebrahimi were both innocent of any crimes. Those aren't even their real names. It was all an elaborate ruse created and executed by Wilton Cross. The truth is that Blackthorn operatives, under his direction, hacked the jet and crashed it into Waikiki. The intent was to use that manufactured terrorist event to convince you, and the president, to outsource the CIA's covert operations to Blackthorn. In my opinion, this was not only an act of homegrown, domestic terrorism but the most heinous act of treason in our nation's history."

"Unbelievable," Senator Holbrook muttered. "Unconscionable."

Seven heads nodded in somber agreement.

"Cross is dead and beyond our reach," Senator Tolan said. "But what about the operatives who collaborated with him to plan and carry out the attack?"

"One of the four Blackthorn operatives killed by police in Los Angeles was in Honolulu at the time of the crash," Healy said. "He stayed in a Diamond Head hotel that would have given him a clear view of Honolulu Airport and Waikiki. We believe he was the one who actually hacked the jet and crashed it."

"Surely there were more than just two people involved in this conspiracy," Tolan snapped. "What about them?"

"We believe there were a little over thirty people directly involved, all working out of Blackthorn's Bethesda headquarters," Healy said. "All but one of them perished in the fire that destroyed the building, which we're telling the public was the result of faulty wiring. But the fire wasn't the only cause of death. Our autopsies have confirmed that they were all shot by one of their own before the blaze."

"Sweet Jesus," Senator Hazeltine said.

"The one survivor managed to give us the broad outlines of the plot in the few hours before she died," Healy said. "Since then, we've managed to fill in most of the blanks."

"What were they doing at that actor's house in Los Angeles?" Hazeltine asked.

"That's one thing we still don't know. Cross must have believed that Ronnie Mancuso figured out that Blackthorn was involved, in some way, with the plane crash or that he presented some other threat to them," Healy said. "But we'll never know for sure because the key players at Blackthorn are dead, the computers were wiped, and Mancuso is crazy."

"When are you releasing a redacted version of your report to the media?" Senator Stowe asked.

"I'm not," Healy said. "As far as I'm concerned, this matter is closed."

"You're doing the right thing," Senator Holbrook said. "The scandal would be devastating for the country."

"It would be devastating for us," Senator Hazeltine said. And the North Carolina politician, more so than anyone in the chamber, had the experience to back up that opinion, having weathered so many corruption scandals of his own.

"It's not his decision to make," Stowe said, gesturing to Healy. "It's ours. We can still reveal what really happened."

"You're right, of course," Tolan said to Stowe. "But we're the only ones left alive that the public can blame for what happened. If the truth comes out, we'll all end up in prison and the president will be impeached . . . and that's if we all get off easy."

"We had nothing to do with crashing that plane," Stowe said. "And we haven't committed any crimes."

"That doesn't make any difference," Tolan said.

The seven men were all experienced politicians. They knew that Tolan, who'd made his name as a showboating Texas prosecutor, was right.

"God help us," Hazeltine said, more to himself than to anybody else in the room. "So how do we explain to the country what happened?"

"We already did," Healy said. "We stick with the brilliantly constructed story that Cross created, and that everyone here and abroad firmly believes."

"But it's all false," Stowe said. "Our government will be taking all kinds of major actions, domestically and overseas, based on a foundation of lies."

"Let me ask you a question, Senator," Healy said to Stowe. "Are the Harakat Ahrar al-Sham al-Islamiyya, and the terrorist groups under their umbrella, our enemies? Do they present a clear and present danger to America?"

"Yes," Stowe said.

"Then who cares if they are blamed for something they didn't do? It just means that some good will come out of this horrific event. The terrorist attack justifies the strong, decisive military action that the president has always wanted to take, and that we all know is necessary to protect our country, but held back doing because the American people haven't had the stomach for it," Healy said. "So you have a choice between a scandal that will cripple our country and turn the public against the government for generations, or gaining widespread public support for an aggressive campaign against terror that will make us all safer. But that, gentlemen, is your decision to make, not mine."

Healy knew the senators would accept his argument, because it was politically expedient and the right thing to do for the country. But it was a hollow victory, one that truly frightened him, because in his heart he knew that this was how it started. This was how a man like him became a man like Wilton Cross.

CHAPTER FORTY-FIVE

If aliens from another planet, perhaps contemplating whether to make friendly contact or to invade our world, were curious about how our culture and government worked and randomly sampled American news broadcasts over the fourteen months that followed the events that July night in Tarzana, these are some of the clips they would have seen: From Nancy O'Dell on *Entertainment Tonight*:

> The former star of *Hollywood & the Vine*, now undergoing psychiatric evaluation, is pleading innocent by reason of insanity to charges of assault with a deadly weapon, reckless driving, and a string of other charges related to the high-speed chase that ended in a shootout at his Tarzana home.

From Jake Tapper on CNN's *The Lead*:

> The Senate has confirmed Michael Healy as director of the CIA, a post he'd previously held on an interim basis after the resignation of Jonas Schepp

in a scandal involving his extramarital affair with an agent's wife. Healy's unanimous confirmation was widely expected after his swift identification and killing of the terrorists responsible for the TransAmerican 976 crash within days of the attack.

From the CBS 2 News in Los Angeles during a live, impromptu news conference held by Tony Petrocelli, the famed criminal attorney representing Ronnie Mancuso, with dozens of media outlets on the courthouse steps:

My client believes that Blackthorn is part of a vast, continuing conspiracy being perpetrated by the global elites to control the world's limited resources for themselves. We will prove that he was the victim of sustained and relentless harassment by Blackthorn that included constant surveillance, the destruction of his home, and an armed assault by trained killers. Is it any wonder that he snapped under that extraordinary pressure?

From Fox News, Shepard Smith reporting as video played of two men emerging bearded and dazed from an underground shelter in Nevada and into the custody of police:

The arrests of two Blackthorn operatives who had been imprisoned for months on Ronnie Mancuso's Nevada property, and the wreckage of one of the infamous "black helicopters" so often referred to by those who believe in the New World Order plot, seem to confirm the actor's claims of a vast conspiracy aligned against him.

From *TMZ*, and reported by some fat guy who looked as if he hadn't bathed in a month:

> Ronnie was released today from Corcoran Mental Hospital after six months of treatment. The first thing he did was go to In-N-Out, where he must have eaten forty double-double burgers. Look at these pictures. He was like one of those competitive eaters you see at a county fair.

From David Muir on *ABC World News Tonight*:

> The remaining assets of Blackthorn Global Security, once the largest private security company in the United States, were sold today to satisfy the terms of the hundred-million-dollar settlement reached with actor Ronnie Mancuso in his lawsuit against the company. As part of the settlement, the company accepted responsibility for destroying the actor's Nevada ranch and an attack on his Los Angeles home last year. The company maintains that actions against Mancuso were carried out by "rogue operatives" under the command of an unnamed executive, one of the thirty-four who were killed in a catastrophic fire at their Bethesda headquarters. The company still faces trial in Los Angeles on a number of criminal charges.

CHAPTER FORTY-SIX

An Excerpt from *Death in the Sky* by Ian Ludlow

The mood in the Blackshadow situation room in midtown Manhattan verged on festive. Clint Straker was dead, tracked to Grand Central Station using the RFID chip in his driver's license. Their assassin had strangled Straker with a garrote in a restroom, left his body in a stall, and put an **OUT OF ORDER** sign on the door. All that they needed to do now was collect the corpse before it was discovered. A containment team was only minutes away.

For the first time in weeks, Dalton Trask could finally relax and truly enjoy his success. The president was on the verge of signing the classified executive order outsourcing the CIA's covert operations to Blackshadow Global Security. The one man who could have stopped it from happening, who'd discovered that it was Blackshadow, and not the Islamic terrorists, that had crashed a plane into downtown Seattle, had just bled out on a toilet. Straker got what he deserved for meddling. He was just one man. He'd never stood a chance against them.

"The team has reached the target." The status update was delivered by Andrea Zane from her command console with her typical urgent intensity, as if the agents were breaching a terrorist compound instead of a men's room in a train station. Her report was also redundant, since the helmet-cam view from the team leader was visible on one of the flat-screens.

The team entered the filthy bathroom and pushed open each stall door, revealing one disgusting, overflowing toilet after another, until they came to one occupied by a man in a dark overcoat. Straker's body was piled on the toilet, his head hanging down, his white shirt and dark slacks drenched in blood.

"They've found him," Andrea said, once again stating the obvious.

"I want to see his face," Dalton said.

The team leader heard Dalton's order in his earpiece and lifted Straker's head by the hair. The gash across Straker's throat gaped at them like an obscene smile.

Except that it wasn't Clint Straker they were looking at. It was another man, wearing dark sunglasses.

"Who the fuck is that?" Dalton roared.

"It's our asset," Andrea said, clearly confused. "But that can't be."

"Why not?" Dalton asked. "You just said that it's him."

"Because he's here in the building," Andrea said, pointing at her screen. "He came through the door ten minutes ago."

To access the building, agents had to pass a retina scan and possess a card key that granted them access to selected areas of the building. Their every move within the building, and every keystroke on their computers, was tracked and logged.

"Take off the dead man's glasses," Dalton said.

The team leader removed the sunglasses from the corpse. One of the dead man's eyeballs was missing. There was a collective gasp as every agent in the room reacted to the gruesome image. Dalton pounded his fist on the console.

Straker was in the building.

"Goddamn it," he said. "Lock down the building. Track the asset's card key and tell me where Straker has been and where he is now."

"He was in your office and now he's—" Andrea began, then looked over her shoulder in horror. Dalton whirled around and saw Clint Straker leaning casually against the wall, an amused smile on his face.

"You've had your eye on me for some time now." Straker tossed a baggie at Dalton, who caught it. The baggie contained the dead assassin's eyeball. "I'm returning it."

Dalton was unperturbed by the eye in the baggie. He held it up, made a show of casually examining it, and set it on the console beside him.

"Bravo, Clint," Dalton said. "You get points for drama and a clever quip but what have you actually accomplished for all of your pitiful efforts?"

"Justice. My old lover Aiko and her thirteen-year-old son were on the plane that you crashed into Seattle." Aiko was the woman who'd taught him the ancient erotic art of 性的超越, or *Seiteki chōetsu*. Now he would never know if the boy was his child. "You killed thousands of innocent people to convince the president to outsource our nation's covert operations to Blackshadow. I'm going to reveal the plot and expose you as the worst traitor in our nation's history."

Dalton laughed. "Even if it was possible for you to leave here alive, which it isn't, you don't have any proof."

"I have a thumb drive full of incriminating files that I just down-loaded from your computer," he said. "The rest will come out in the investigation."

"What investigation?"

"Into the bombing," Straker said and lobbed a hand grenade into the center of the room.

CHAPTER FORTY-SEVEN

The crowd that came to see Ian Ludlow at Union Bay Books on that Saturday night was standing room only, perhaps because Seattle figured so prominently in his new thriller. The cover of *Death in the Sky* was a vivid illustration of Clint Straker's silhouette toting a rocket launcher, charging toward the reader against the backdrop of a plane crashing into the Space Needle in an enormous fireball.

But Ian was disappointed by the turnout because the one person he really hoped to see wasn't there. He walked outside into the hot summer night.

"Shall I take you back to your hotel?" asked Gwen, his author escort. She was a graduate student in the University of Washington English Department who ferried novelists around town so she could pitch them her book. It was a civil war allegory set on a planet of unicorns, zebras, and horses.

"No, thank you. It's so nice out, I think I'll walk," Ian said. "See you tomorrow at the mystery bookstore."

"Would you like to meet early for coffee?" she asked. "I can show you my first chapter. Clint Straker shares more in common with unicorns than you might think."

"I'm sure you're right," he said. "Maybe another time."

She smiled, got into her Prius, and drove off. Ian watched her go.

"Why are you so fucking polite?" a familiar voice asked. "Tell her where to stick her unicorn. That's what Clint Straker would do."

Ian smiled as Margo stepped out of the shadows. "I'm not Clint Straker."

"You could have fooled me," Margo said. "How did the signing go?"

"It was great. I may need to ice my wrist."

"From inscribing so many books or because you're practicing Ronnie's method for staying healthy?"

"Both," Ian said and he hugged her. She squeezed him tight. "I'm glad you came."

"What else did I have to do? My dog-sitting business has dried up, all because of one negative Yelp review."

"You left the dogs alone with a pile of food, a bucket of water, and a corpse impaled with a fireplace poker."

"One time!" Margo said. "How often is that likely to happen?"

Ian laughed and gestured to the bookstore. "Why didn't you come for the reading and the Q and A?"

"Living it was enough. I'm still suffering from PTSD."

"Really?" Ian said.

"No, I'm fine. What we went through forced me to get my shit together. I'm focusing entirely on my music now," she said. "I'm writing songs. I play three nights a week at a steak house here in town and I do a lot of weddings, bar mitzvahs, that kind of thing."

"That's how Rihanna started," Ian said.

"I have a hard time picturing Rihanna singing 'Hava Nagila.'"

"I have a hard time picturing you singing 'Hava Nagila.'"

That's when they both became aware of two men approaching on either side of them, both in business suits and wearing earpieces.

"Mr. Ludlow," the first man said. "Ms. French."

"Can you please come with us?" the second man said.

Ian and Margo shared a look and then let themselves be escorted to a limousine parked on the corner. The first man opened the back door for them and motioned for them to go inside. Margo gave Ian a nervous look.

"He said 'please,'" Ian said. "That's a good sign."

"And it's a limo, not a hearse."

"So there's no reason to worry." Ian took a deep breath and got in. Margo followed.

The agent closed the door. They found themselves sitting across from CIA Director Michael Healy, who had Ian's new book on his lap. Healy acknowledged Ian with a nod and smiled at Margo.

"I'm sure Mr. Ludlow knows who I am, since he writes so much about espionage and government conspiracies," Healy said to Margo. "But you may not. I'm Michael Healy, director of the Central Intelligence Agency."

He offered her his hand. She shook it. "Does this car have machine gun turrets and ejector seats?"

"No, I'm afraid not," he said.

"That's no fun," she said.

Healy shifted his attention to Ian. "I read your book. Scary stuff."

"Most of it's true but you already know that," Ian said. "The only thing I made up was the security company's motive for crashing the plane because I didn't know the real one."

"The whole notion is preposterous," Healy said. "The government would never outsource covert operations to the private sector."

"Okay," Margo said. "So why did Blackthorn crash the jet?"

Healy gave her a hard look. "They didn't."

"Yeah, yeah, that's the official line but it's just us boys in here," Margo said. "You can tell us the truth. What place could be more secure than the CIA director's limo? Or are you worried the car is bugged?"

Healy ignored her and focused his attention again on Ian. "I know it was you on the phone with Cross. I know everything."

"I would hope so," Ian said. "It would be a sad commentary on the CIA if you didn't."

"And if I didn't, I would have known after reading your book," Healy said. "You exposed yourself. That wasn't very smart."

Ian shrugged. "It's my failing. I'm a storyteller. I couldn't resist telling a good story."

"The president appreciates that you chose to tell your story as fiction. So do I. You did the right thing for your country."

"I wasn't being patriotic," Ian said. "I don't think the country would be too thrilled if they knew that what happened in Hawaii was my idea."

"That's why I'm here," Healy said. "Your fiction has an uncanny way of becoming fact. We could use people with imagination at the CIA."

Ian laughed. "Are you offering me a job?"

"How would you like to become Clint Straker?" Healy asked. "You'd still be a writer, traveling all over the world researching your international thrillers, but you'd also be working for us. It's the perfect cover."

"Author by day? Secret agent by night?"

"Something like that," Healy said.

"You can't be serious." Margo glared at Healy and then turned to Ian. "Have you forgotten that this is how you got into trouble before?"

"Relax," Ian said. "I didn't say I was going to do it."

"You didn't say no, either."

That was true. He didn't.

ACKNOWLEDGMENTS

I want to thank former FBI agents Jim Clemente and Mark Safarik, former police officers Paul Bishop and Robin Burcell, airline pilots Mark Danielson and Shawn Kelly, and Dr. D. P. Lyle for their detailed answers to my dumb questions. I used and abused what they told me to fit the diabolical needs of my story, so any errors you discover are entirely my fault and quite possibly intentional.

ABOUT THE AUTHOR

Photo © 2013 Roland Scarpa

Lee Goldberg is a two-time Edgar Award and two-time Shamus Award nominee and the #1 *New York Times* bestselling author of more than thirty novels, including *King City*, *The Walk*, fifteen Monk mysteries, and the internationally bestselling Fox & O'Hare books (*The Heist*, *The Chase*, *The Job*, *The Scam*, and *The Pursuit*), cowritten with Janet Evanovich. He has also written and/or produced scores of TV shows, including *Diagnosis Murder*, *SeaQuest*, *Monk*, and *The Glades*. As an international television consultant, he has advised networks and studios in Canada, France, Germany, Spain, China, Sweden, and the Netherlands on the creation, writing, and production of episodic television series. You can find more information about Lee and his work at www.leegoldberg.com.